'That is a pict

'So I've been sleep
the past nine mont

'I'm not married,' James said. 'The thought of adultery leaves me with a very sour taste in my mouth. My wife died ten years ago.'

'I had no idea,' Claire whispered. 'I'm sorry.'

'Claire, let me make one thing absolutely clear between us. I want you. But if you're looking for commitment, then you're looking at the wrong man. My capacity for love was well and truly expended on Olivia.'

Dear Reader

Summer might be drawing to an end—but don't despair! This month's selection of exciting love stories is guaranteed to bring back a little sunshine! Why not let yourself be transported to the beauty of a Caribbean paradise—or perhaps you'd prefer the exotic mystery of Egypt? All in the company of a charming and devastatingly handsome hero, naturally! Of course, you don't have to go abroad to find true romance—and when you're a Mills & Boon reader you don't even need to step outside your front door! Just relax with this book, and you'll see what we mean . . .

The Editor

Cathy Williams is Trinidadian and was brought up on the twin islands of Trinidad and Tobago. She was awarded a scholarship to study in Britain, and came to Exeter University in 1975 to continue her studies into the great loves of her life: languages and literature. It was there that Cathy met her husband, Richard. Since they married Cathy has lived in England, originally in the Thames Valley but now in the Midlands. Cathy and Richard have two small daughters.

Recent titles by the same author:

UNWILLING SURRENDER

SHADOWS OF YESTERDAY

BY
CATHY WILLIAMS

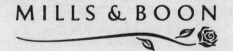

MILLS & BOON LIMITED
ETON HOUSE, 18-24 PARADISE ROAD
RICHMOND, SURREY TW9 1SR

*MILLS & BOON and the Rose Device
are trademarks of the publisher.*

*First published in Great Britain 1994
by Mills & Boon Limited*

© Cathy Williams 1994

*Australian copyright 1994   Philippine copyright 1994
This edition 1994*

ISBN 0 263 78626 9

*Set in Times Roman 10 on 12 pt.
01-9409-55794 C*

Made and printed in Great Britain

CHAPTER ONE

CLAIRE'S hand was trembling. There had to be some kind of mistake, some kind of dreadful mistake.

That didn't go very far towards making her feel any better, though, and she subsided into the leather chair by the window with a sick, faint feeling.

She leaned her head against the palm of her hand, her eyes flicking around the small, exquisite study, but not really seeing it at all.

She would have to wait for him. He was due back any minute now, and everything would be neatly explained.

She breathed a little sigh of relief at the thought of that and settled back in the chair, her eyes half closed. Outside, it was pitch dark, and freezing cold. It was March, but a bitterly cold March, with forecasters reminding them every day that England had not seen a spring like this for decades.

Inside, however, the study was warm, as was the entire place. That had been one of the first things that had struck her when she had started working at Frilton Manor nearly a year ago. This was not one of those splendid country mansions which were breathtakingly beautiful to look at but dismally archaic inside. No, James Forrester was a man who liked his creature comforts, and he was wealthy enough to ensure that every one of them was indulged at the snap of a finger.

Not for him vast, unheated rooms, threadbare carpets and unflattering portraits of deceased ancestors. The place was entirely heated, the carpets were luxuriously deep-piled and the unflattering ancestral portraits were confined to the gallery in the left wing. In their place an assortment of mostly Impressionistic masterpieces adorned the walls.

It wasn't so long ago that she had wandered through the rooms, lost in speechless wonder. Everything had been a revelation of good taste.

Right now, with that little seven-by-five photo clutched in her hand, she felt as though all that impressionable, youthful ingenuousness had finally been killed off and she had to insist to herself that she was being prematurely pessimistic, that James would be able to explain away that cool blonde, with her arm linked through his, dressed in an ivory suit and holding a bunch of some unidentifiable flowers against her stomach.

Next to him, with his impossibly impressive, dark and slightly cruel good looks, she was like an ice maiden, tall, pale and with a peculiar, frozen beauty of her own.

Her fingers tightened on the photo and she found that she was breathing quickly, nervously, like a scared wild animal that had wandered into an unsuspected trap.

Maybe, she thought with a rare stab of bitterness, this fear was simply a culmination of what she had been feeling, deep inside, for the past nine months, ever since she had begun sleeping with him. What, after all, had she to offer a man like James Forrester—someone with power, wealth and looks, a man who could crook a finger and have any woman he wanted running to him? She was no great beauty with her uneventful brown hair, blue eyes and pale complexion, a brunette who couldn't tan, of all things.

And she certainly did not inhabit his rarefied world of the rich, the privileged and the powerful. Her roots were humble ones, her parents both teachers and both now retired, safely tucked away in deepest Devon, a thousand light-years away from stocks and shares and the cut-throat concrete jungle which was his life blood.

Which brought her to the photo and the inevitable question it raised: where was their relationship going? She was desperately in love with him, and she knew that he was fond of her and was attracted to her, that much had always been obvious in the flare in his eyes whenever they were together, but there it ended. He did not want commitment. That was something which had needed no explanation. It was evident in every caress, every touch that was unaccompanied by the declarations of love she longed to hear. It was as intangible but as powerfully present as the air she breathed.

And for the past nine months she had, with increasing unease, played the game by his rules; but now, she thought, staring at the photo in front of her, things were going to change. She was not going to become one of those women who spent years miserably devoted to a man who had no intention of offering anything beyond the occasional meal out and sex on demand.

God only knew why she had stuck it out for so long. It was completely out of character. She frowned, and in the dim recesses of her mind she wondered whether there wasn't some inevitable logic to her behaviour after all. She had had boyfriends in the past, but they had never measured up to the hopelessly impossible standards which she had set in her imagination. I've spent my life searching for a fairy-tale, she thought bitterly, looking for some dark, dramatic knight in shining armour. How could college boys and local lads ever have filled the role? None of them had fuelled her imagination.

With James it had been different from the word go. He had been altogether different from the sort of boys she had been accustomed to, as different as a shark was from a goldfish. Underneath that sophisticated exterior, he possessed a rapier mind and a lean, predatory sex appeal which she had never in her life come across.

She had taken one look at him and she had been bowled over. Nothing in her life had prepared her for that heady rush of excitement which his mere presence could arouse in her, and she had done nothing to protect herself.

But then, looking back on it now, she had not realised just how quickly she would become engulfed, until he filled her every waking moment, until she only seemed to breathe, to come alive, when he was around. She had given everything of herself to him, without ever really stopping to realise that he had given precious little in return.

What a fool I've been, she thought with an angry stab of pain, throwing myself into bed with him, lapping up the crumbs he's tossed out like a thirsty dog at a bowl of water. Where has all my pride gone?

Little wonder she had never mentioned him to her parents. Some instinct must have warned her that their relationship, if it could be called that, was far from satisfactory, and her parents would have had a fit if they had known what an emotional mess she was in. They were old-fashioned people with old-fashioned principles, and sleeping with a virtual stranger did not, by any stretch of the imagination, fit into the category of upholding old-fashioned principles.

All these things had been fermenting away in her head for some time now, but it was only here, sitting in this armchair, clutching this photo, that they all came together and filled her with horror. How could she have been so stupid?

It had been sheer cowardice, she realised, sticking with James. It had been an intense, addictive relationship from the start, and whenever common sense had shown the slightest sign of putting in an appearance, she had quickly ushered it away because just the thought of never seeing that hard-boned, arrogant, good-looking face again, of never knowing that dry, incisive humour, had terrified her.

She was so lost in her thought that she was unaware of the door opening until he filled the doorway, a tall, looming figure that made her heart skip a beat. For a second, she had to blink because it was almost as if the intensity of her thoughts had managed to conjure him up in front of her, then she began to feel that familiar pounding in her chest, that weak-kneed craving she had whenever he was around, and she had to steel every nerve in her body not to respond to him.

If he was surprised to see her, he didn't show it. He came into the room, moving with the lithe grace of someone whose body was finely tuned to perfection, and discarded his coat, loosening his tie and tugging at it so that he could undo the top button of his shirt.

'What,' he said at last, walking towards her and giving her a long, appraising look, 'are you doing here? I thought that you would have been safely tucked up in bed in the cottage.' He bent down, reaching out to support himself on the arms of the chair, and she had a dizzy sensation of drowning.

This was how it always was. He could always somehow reduce her to a mindless, obedient female, but this time it wasn't going to work, this time she wasn't going to allow herself to get swept into that vortex of passion that he could generate without even really seeming to try.

'I knew that you would be back around now,' Claire muttered, grateful that the study was in virtual darkness. The lamp on the desk was switched on, but that was the only source of light, not enough for him to detect the sharp red colour that had flowed up to her cheeks.

'So you came to greet me,' he murmured softly. He reached out and lazily trailed one finger along her neck, under the thin material of her blouse. She had earlier discarded her thick blue jumper, and now she wished desperately that she hadn't. It would have provided a barrier against those long, sensual fingers. Her body felt as though it had been frozen, and she was hardly aware of him undoing the buttons of her shirt until he slipped his hand under, to caress the full swell of her breast, his thumb moving erotically over the tight bud of her nipple.

She gasped with a mixture of astonishment and un-willing arousal, and her body jerked into life. She pushed his hand away and wriggled frantically to get up, but he was still leaning over her and he coiled his fingers into her hair, forcing her to remain where she was.

His face had hardened at her unexpected reaction, but he was still in control, although he wasn't pleased, that much was evident from his tight expression. She felt a swift dart of pleasure and very slowly but very pointedly she began to button up her shirt, taking her time and hoping that he couldn't make out just how nervous she was.

'Playing games, Claire?' he asked coolly, straightening up and walking across to the mahogany bar in the corner of the study. He poured himself a drink and turned to face her.

'No,' she answered, over-loud. 'When have I ever played games with you?' Her hands were still trembling and she sat on them, feeling the photo under her thigh and curling her fingers around it.

'Then would you care to explain your presence here? It's been one hell of a day and I don't relish rounding it off by trying to guess what's going on in that head of yours.' He switched on the overhead light and she blinked, dazzled and taken aback. She didn't want to see that dark, arrogant face any more than she wanted him to see hers, and with the light switched on she felt as though there was nowhere to hide.

'Perhaps,' she said, with a hysterical edge to her voice, 'I came for conversation. Having a relationship with someone does involve the odd bit of conversation, doesn't it? Or maybe I'm asking for too much from you.'

'What the hell has got into you?' he asked grimly. 'If you've decided to come up to the house, at eleven-thirty at night, to subject me to a monologue on the values of conversation, then it can wait. I'm damned tired and I have no intention of indulging this unexpected bout of temper.' He gulped down the remainder of his drink and then slammed the glass on to the desk, making her jump.

'I want to talk to you!' she said in a burst, sliding her eyes away from his because she knew that he had the ability to reduce her to a gibbering wreck if he decided.

'By all means.' He began walking towards the door, undoing his shirt.

'What are you doing?' she asked, springing up and following him, half running to keep up as he strode into the massive hall, then up the winding staircase towards his bedroom.

This is ridiculous, she thought. She had sat there for well over two hours, clutching that wretched photo, armed and prepared for confrontation, and here she was now, racing along behind him like some damned serf while he casually undressed along the way. By the time he arrived at his bedroom door, he was tugging his white shirt out of the waistband of his trousers.

She stopped where she was, by the door, knowing that his bedroom was just about the last place in the world where she should be having a serious conversation. But maybe, she thought with unaccustomed cynicism, that was his ploy. He was damned shrewd, shrewd enough to know that by bringing her here he would immediately have the advantage. Hadn't he always had the advantage in the bedroom?

He stripped off his shirt and tossed it on the chair by the window, not looking in her direction.

His body had always fascinated her, with its sensual, powerful lines and light bronze colouring so unusual in the English. In one of his rare moments of confidence, he had told her that that had to do with the fact that his mother had been Italian, a wild, dark-haired beauty who had swept his stolid English father off his feet, much to his relatives' disgust. The only thing English about me, he had assured her, is my name, and she could believe that because there was something untamed about him.

'I don't intend,' he informed her, still without looking in her direction, walking towards the marble en-suite bathroom and dressing-room, 'to shout to you from the bathroom, so you can either step over that threshold or else whatever you have to say will have to wait until another, more appropriate time.'

He turned on the shower and Claire reluctantly closed the bedroom door behind her and followed him to the dressing-room.

He had turned on the shower and through the open door she could see him getting undressed until he was completely naked. He was making no effort to continue their conversation. Either he was totally incurious about what she had to say or else he was simply waiting until she was forced to break the silence.

Claire took a few steps towards the bathroom but she didn't enter, and she refused to give in to the temptation to stare at the sleek, strong body, hazy behind the smoked shower-door. She deliberately turned away and stared in the opposite direction. It was a dramatic bedroom, full of deep reds and golds, with an eighteenth-century four-poster bed dominating everything. Quite out of character from the rest of the place, which relied on muted colours to create a feeling of refined good taste. It had always struck her as a fitting background for someone as sensuous as James.

'Still pretending to be a shrinking violet?' he whispered from next to her, and she jumped, turning around to stare at him. His hair was damp and he was wearing nothing apart from a thick beige towel wrapped precariously around his waist. The shower had obviously refreshed him, though. He was in a better mood, not as abrupt and biting as when he had first walked into the study.

'Still set on talking?' he asked in the same low voice, and he gave her a smile of such devastating charm that the breath caught in her throat. 'Or should we postpone the conversation in favour of something less cerebral?' His fingers curled into her hair and he drew her forward, tilting her face up to him. Her lips parted, an unconscious reaction, and he covered them with his own. She felt him harden, aroused, against her and she placed the palms of her hands on his chest and pushed him away. He stepped back, surprised and irritated.

He *would* be surprised, she thought, and irritated. She had never rejected him before. On the contrary, she had yielded to him like a flower bending in the wind, allowing him to dictate her responses, the eager novice so willing to be taught. The thought of it was enough to make her feel ill.

'Well,' he said, turning away and unhitching the towel from his waist, throwing it across a chair then rummaging through the chest of drawers to extract a pair of silk boxer shorts, which he slipped on before turning to her, 'get it off your chest. You're standing there like a virgin about to be raped. I don't think I can stand the suspense of wondering what you have to say that's of such great importance.'

'Really?' Claire said flatly. 'You don't look like a man who's dying of suspense. In fact, you don't look as though you give a damn about what I have to say.'

That outburst surprised him even more. He folded his arms across his chest and stared at her as though she had taken leave of her senses.

This was the first time that she had ever confronted him. He was not a man to encourage confrontations. There was a steel-hard core to him that made you think twice before you decided to cross him. Now, she was beginning to wish that she had never begun on this route. He was making her nervous, staring at her like that with those dramatic, shuttered green eyes, his arms folded, like someone who was temporarily willing to be indulgent, but not for very long. She licked her lips and told herself that she had nothing to be scared of. She had slept with this man, and besides, she had every right to ask him whatever she chose to. He could hardly kill her just because he didn't care for the question.

'Well?' he prompted silkily. 'I'm all ears.'

Claire took a deep, steadying breath and stretched out her hand with the photo. 'I'd like to know about this,' she said quietly.

He stepped forward and took the picture. He stared at it, then he looked up at her, his eyes as hard as diamonds.

'And where did you get this?'

'In the drawer of your study,' Claire said defiantly. 'I was doing some artwork at the cottage and my paper supply ran out. I thought that you might have had some foolscap up here. I know you sometimes work from your study, and I didn't think that you would mind...' Her voice trailed off and she realised that her courage was beginning to desert her. When she had been angry, it had been easy to face the thought of confronting him, but now she was no longer angry, she was scared stiff, and she had no idea what to say next. Every word was like taking one step further on molten lava.

There was a long, unbroken silence and finally he said in a cold voice, 'I would have locked that bureau if I had suspected that you would feel free to come up here and rummage through it.'

'I was not rummaging through it,' Claire defended hotly. 'But how else would I have found the paper if I hadn't...?'

'Had a good, long look at everything else in there,' he finished for her and she went scarlet, even though what he was implying was far from the truth. She hadn't been nosing around. That sort of thing simply wasn't in her nature.

'I wasn't even looking in the drawer,' she said angrily. 'I stuck my hand in...'

'And lo and behold, what should it chance upon but this?' He threw the photo on the bed where it landed face-down.

'Will you let me finish?' she asked tightly. 'Yes, I pulled it out, and yes, I looked at it, of course, I'm only human after all. I *thought*,' she added with a trace of sarcasm, 'that you might want to provide an explanation.'

He was beginning to look dangerously angry, and her eyes widened in apprehension as he took a step towards her.

'I can't imagine why you would think any such thing,' he said in a soft voice that carried a hint of distaste in it. 'I didn't realise that I *owed* you anything, least of all an explanation about something that's really none of your business.'

That hurt, but she wasn't going to let him see that. The man in front of her wasn't the James that she had fallen in love with. This was a stranger, a cold, menacing stranger.

'We've slept together,' she began, and he gave a bark of laughter.

'And?'

'And,' she stuttered in confusion, 'and I would have thought, I would have imagined ... I mean when two people sleep together, they usually share things ...' As soon as the words were uttered, she realised how ridiculous they sounded. There was nothing cosy about their relationship, it wasn't an ordinary, run-of-the mill situation where two people shared their bed and their hearts. It was wild, and obsessive, and ultimately, she knew now, fatal, at least for her.

'I always knew that you were far too young for me,' he said coolly. 'Because, my dear Claire, we made love, that does not entitle you to scour my private life.'

'But I *am* your private life!'

'You flatter yourself.' He turned away and she blinked rapidly, fighting down the sting of tears.

He moved across to stand at the window, half turned away from her, an impressive animal without an ounce of scruple, and she wanted to rush across to him and tear his eyes out.

'Didn't I mean *anything* to you?' she asked, trying with great difficulty to maintain some semblance of self-control.

His shoulders stiffened and he remained silent for so long that she began to wonder whether he had heard her question. Not that she was inclined to repeat it. After all, it didn't take a genius to deduce the answer from that telling, prolonged silence.

'What do you want me to say to that?' he asked, facing her, half sitting on the window ledge.

Yes! she wanted to scream at him, I want you to say yes! I want you to say that you're as crazy about me as I am about you! I want you to declare undying love and fidelity!

'You don't have to say anything,' she managed to inform him. 'I'm not stupid, whatever you might think. I can read between the lines.'

'I never encouraged you to think...'

'I know. And I don't think...I don't expect anything from you. I would, however, still like to know what that picture was all about, not that you *owe* me anything, as you've told me in no uncertain terms.'

'That,' he said without a change of tone, 'is a picture of my wife.'

Claire blanched, then turned bright red. Her body felt as though it was on fire. What had she expected? she asked herself. It was obviously a wedding photo, wasn't it? If she had been a bit more realistic instead of hiding behind some stupid pretence that he could explain it away, she would have acknowledged that.

'So I've been sleeping with a married man for the past nine months,' she said through still lips. 'Have you any more surprises in store for me, James? Perhaps you're an escaped convict and this house doesn't really belong to you at all!' Her voice had risen sharply. 'You've managed to keep your wife a secret for the past nine months. Where is she, anyway? Locked away in one of the bedrooms somewhere? Or does she hide away and let you get on with your little affairs on the side? Tell me, James, I'm dying to know!'

He moved swiftly towards her and grasped her hands, pinning them to her sides so that she couldn't escape.

'You're hysterical,' he said harshly, dragging her towards the bed and throwing her on it. She made to get up but he forestalled that by trapping her with his arms, so she lay there passively, lowering her eyes so that he couldn't see the mutiny in them.

'Can you blame me?' she asked viciously.

'I'm not married,' he said. 'The thought of adultery leaves me with a very sour taste in my mouth. My wife died ten years ago.'

'I had no idea,' Claire whispered. 'I'm sorry.' There was a pause while she fought down the accusations she had hurled at him. 'How is it that you never mentioned her?'

There was no softening in his expression as he looked down at her.

'I didn't see the need,' he said in a smooth, hard voice. 'Claire, let me make one thing absolutely clear between us. What we have is physical. I want you. But if you're looking for commitment, then you're looking in the wrong place, at the wrong man. My capacity for love was well and truly expended on Olivia.'

Olivia. Lovely name. It suited that blonde, imperious beauty. Not forgetting tragic. Tragic beauty, she thought—the worst kind. How on earth could you fight the past?

'You can't mean that,' she said without thinking.

'Don't play the crusader with me, Claire. I'm quite happy to enjoy what we have, but don't waste your time with me if marriage is what you're after. Is it?'

'Did I ever imply that?' she asked weakly, averting her eyes. She was breathing quickly, her breasts rising and falling.

'Good,' he said, 'because it would be so unfortunate if what we have was forced to end prematurely, wouldn't it?' He pushed aside her blouse, exposing her breasts and slowly, tenderly he began to caress them.

He had been her first and only lover. He had taught her to make love, giving her enjoyment until she was confident enough to return it to him. Her body responded to him now with an almost reflex rush of desire. The peaks of her nipples hardened, ready to receive the warm wetness of his mouth. Her mind seemed to shut down completely, so that when his lips finally did encircle her swollen nipples it took a while for coherent thought to resurface. But resurface it did, and she wriggled against him, pushing him back, desperate to get away.

This time, though, he was less willing to release her. He pinned her arms down and she immediately stopped squirming. There was no point. He was strong, she knew that from experience, and in a physical contest he would always be the winner, so why waste energy in trying to fight him? He couldn't restrain her forever, and the minute his hands were off her she'd be out of here.

Her passivity annoyed him yet further.

'It's no good,' she said flatly. 'You can strip me until I'm completely naked, but you can't make me want you.'

'Can't I?' There was disbelief in his voice and she watched him angrily from under her lashes. 'Shall we put that to the test?'

His eyes raked over her, and it was like being branded by a hot iron. Who, she thought, was she trying to kid? She wanted him now just like she had always wanted him. It was an illness, a craving that was bigger than her. The thought of him looking at her nudity, caressing her bare breasts with his eyes, was enough to bring hectic colour to her cheeks, even though he was no longer touching her.

'If that makes you happy,' she said with a careless shrug, and she could tell from the stiffening of his body that she was really beginning to get under his skin. She didn't know whether to feel afraid or elated. 'You can subdue me easily, but what does that prove except that you're stronger than I am? And sure, if you make love to me, I'll probably be aroused by you, but just because my body might respond it doesn't mean that my mind is as well.' Anger, bitterness, hurt had loosened her tongue and, now that she had started talking, it was as if she could no longer stop herself. She had stored up nine months of passionate, unbridled, frustrated love, and all that was pouring out of her in an un-stoppable torrent.

'You're so sure of yourself, aren't you, James?' she asked in a high-pitched voice. 'Have you ever run into any obstacles in your life? I doubt it. You've sailed through life assuming that it's your right that everyone bends to your will.' She gave an uncontrolled, acid laugh and sat up, smoothing her appearance with trembling fingers. 'I was a fool to ever be taken in by that charm of yours!' She lifted her face rebelliously to his, her chin jutting forward with unaccustomed aggression. 'You play with women, don't you? Did it amuse you to play with me? Did my virginity turn you on?' She had gone beyond the point of rational thought. She was fired by the biting pain of knowing that the man she loved belonged to his dead wife.

'You turned me on,' he said harshly, the green of his eyes glittering like a cat's, 'and yes, your virginity was part of you. Would you prefer it if I lied? Would you like me to tell you that I loved you? Would you like me to feed you stories about eternal bliss?' She was staring up at him, her eyes as wide as saucers. 'Dammit, woman!' He stood up and began pacing the room, like a caged animal, raking his fingers through his hair and she watched him with unwilling, greedy fascination.

Of course she should leave, but something kept her nailed to the bed.

'Don't look at me like that!' he commanded, standing still and fixing her with those amazing eyes.

'Like what?'

'You told me that you never played games with me. Well, I never played them with you. I never offered you what I couldn't provide.'

The atmosphere was thick with tension and she looked away hurriedly, physically unable to outstare him even though she would have liked to. She felt as though she had opened a door and found a nightmare behind it. Her sister, she knew, would have been proud. Jackie was seven years older than her, and she had never met James Forrester, but that hadn't stopped her from lecturing on his unsuitability.

'I know you,' she had told Claire early on in her relationship. 'You're too green for a man like that. You're a dreamer, you've always been a dreamer. Even when you were a teenager and you should have been out having fun, you locked yourself away in your bedroom with your books and your fantasies. Right now you're a novelty for him because he's accustomed to other types of women, sophisticated women with carefully applied make-up and designer wardrobes. You're young and fresh and just so damned *innocent*, but he'll tire of you and when he does you can be sure that he won't think twice about sending you on your way.'

Claire had listened because she loved her sister, but she hadn't taken the slightest bit of notice of the warnings. The pull he had over her was too powerful to allow her any room for reason.

'No, you never offered me anything that you couldn't provide,' she repeated dully. Her intense anger had evaporated and she felt drained and hopeless. 'Thank you so much for that, at least. How good you've been, what a true gentleman.'

His lips tightened and he stared at her as though he would have liked to have shaken her and was only controlling himself with extreme difficulty.

She stood up and walked slowly towards the door. Inside, she felt dead and lifeless. This was the first time that she had ever exploded like this with James, with anyone for that matter. She was not a girl who liked arguments; she had always preferred to take the path of least possible resistance. Perhaps because her parents had so seldom argued, quarrelling perturbed her, made her feel awkward and uncomfortable.

'I can't compete with your wife,' she said quietly, her hand on the doorknob. 'I just wish that you'd liked me enough to tell me about her sooner.'

'Liking,' he said coolly, not trying to stop her from leaving, 'had nothing to do with it.'

'How can you still be so affected by the past?' she heard herself ask, desperately, and the shutters clamped back down over his eyes. She preferred him cold, angry, biting, anything but this closed expression that gave her no inkling as to what he was thinking.

He took a step towards her and she cringed back, like a wounded animal.

'Is it ever really possible to escape the past?' he asked smoothly, an acid, humourless smile on his face. 'You're a child. I should never have given in to my impulses; I should have left you to play out your little infatuation.'

'Thank you for that,' she whispered, hating herself for loving this man when he was capable of being so utterly hateful. 'But it's not too late to be rid of me.' She opened the door and stepped out into the corridor. 'I'm leaving now and this is the last you'll see of me, so you can carry on with your life and I can finish playing out all my stupid, childish games.'

She shut the door behind her and flew down the corridor, gaining momentum as she ran down the staircase as if there were baying hounds behind her, when in fact he hadn't made even the slightest effort to stop her in her tracks.

Why should he? she thought as she let herself out of the front door. I've only ever been a little bit of fun on the side. He's still in love with Olivia.

CHAPTER TWO

CLAIRE had been only just twenty when she'd met James Forrester.

It had been on one of those depressing winter days when the sun never seemed to rise and darkness fell like a shutter in mid-afternoon. Not a day to be wondering for how much longer she would be able to afford the rent on her poky bedroom in the house she shared with three other girls. Money was low and she was loath to mention the problem to her parents because they would immediately insist on helping her out. Even at twenty, they still thought of her as their baby, their little girl who should be protected.

Not to mention the fact that her parents would have been hard pushed to bail her out of her financial troubles. Her father wasn't exactly rolling in money and although they had some savings, it was common knowledge to both their daughters that this money was being carefully put aside for a rainy day.

So she had continued scouring the newspapers, anxiously looking for jobs and wondering whether she would have been better off remaining in London instead of moving to Berkshire where the rent was much lower and where she had optimistically thought that the job situation would be good.

Six weeks out of work, with nothing hopeful on the horizon, was not doing much for her self-confidence, though.

Two of the girls who rented the house with her bluntly told her that she ought to find a job as a secretary, invest her time in a short typing course which would reap its rewards in the years to come; after all, they earned good money, thank you very much, working as secretaries in two of the larger companies in nearby Reading.

But Claire had not jumped at their suggestion. She had worked hard for her art diploma and to throw away everything she had studied for, to abandon her love of art in favour of a nine-to-five routine in front of a type-writer, did not hold much appeal.

But as she had sat at the kitchen table, scanning the job columns, she had been forced to admit that a love of art was not going to pay the bills.

She also doubted whether her landlord would smilingly accept her need to be creative and overlook the little matter of unpaid rent on his house. He was sharklike at the best of times, and she shuddered at the prospect of trying to engage his sympathy for her cause.

Then she had spotted it. Just when she had been about to crumple the newspaper into a ball and admit defeat. Cleaner wanted, it said, excellent rates of pay for the right person. More to the point, she would be working at Frilton Manor.

She had telephoned the number on the advertisement immediately and had been given an interview only hours later.

And she just knew that this was going to work out. She would be earning money, she would be able to keep herself in room and board until the sort of job she really wanted came along, and, best of all, she would be sur-rounded by all that magnificent beauty at the manor—because it would be beautiful, she could tell just from what she had seen of it from the outside: large, imposing, set on a hill and looking down on the rest of the world with a mixture of grandeur and contempt.

She had been right. She had got the job because, she was told by the head housekeeper, she looked trustworthy and she could start the following morning.

Then she had been shown around the manor, or rather part of it because some of the rooms were closed and besides it was simply too massive to be viewed in the length of time available.

Claire had been awestruck. Her own family home had been a small three-bedroomed cottage, with just enough space for four people and a dog, and even the dog had a tendency to get underfoot now and again. She couldn't imagine what it must be like to actually live somewhere as vast as Frilton Manor.

'Are there any children?' she had asked the housekeeper, who had given her a curious look.

'Children? Of course not. The master lives here on his own. Not that he gets down here that often. His work is in London, you see, and he has a flat there, but when he does come here it has to be in spotless condition. It's not that he's a stickler for cleanliness,' she had hurriedly continued, 'but I am.' She looked around her proudly. 'There's four of us whose job it is to make sure things keep ticking over, and I do the cooking as well when the master is at home. George, that's my husband, is responsible for the garden. He employs some local lads to help him. The master trusts us,' she said, holding her head high, making Claire smile, 'we're responsible for who works here and we have to be careful. There's a lot of valuables in this house. The antiques, the pictures.' She made a sweeping gesture, and Claire nodded appreciatively.

'Priceless, I should think,' she contributed helpfully, but she was really only half listening to what the house-keeper was saying. Her eyes were roaming around the place in open delight, taking in the graceful curves of the staircase which dominated the massive hallway, sweeping up to branch into two long corridors which formed a huge square and off which the bedrooms were located.

And on the walls were a mind-boggling array of paintings, some of them portraits, others landscapes, all original. For an art lover, it was sheer heaven.

There was even a magnificent library, which she had briefly seen, and which had lived up to all her expec-tations of what a library ought to be like in a grand, old house. Dark, with rich deep colours, and sombre paintings on the walls, and an impressive display of books, most hardbound, but some, she was interested to see, modern classics.

'Of course priceless!' the housekeeper said haughtily, making Claire smile again.

They were back in the hallway when the telephone began ringing, and the housekeeper hurried off, leaving her to let herself out. But Claire didn't immediately. She remained where she was, absorbing the wonderful state-liness of the place, loving the beauty and the stillness of it.

She would telephone her sister this evening and tell her all about her stroke of good fortune, although she knew what her sister would say. Damn dull, working in a great big place like that. It's not good for you, you need to get out more, mix with young people, not do a cleaning job in a mausoleum.

Jackie had not wanted her to leave London. She was a firm believer in the city life and she had been convinced

that with a little more personal guidance Claire would
have broken out of her shell and become less introverted. She had said as much, and Claire had listened
with a half-smile, not liking to say that the bright lights
were not for her. She had found London oppressive and
overcrowded and she just couldn't work herself up to
feel enthusiastic about the nightclubs and the wine bars
and the never-ending round of social engagements which
her sister seemed to delight in. There had to be more to
life than a routine job in a claustrophobic city. She had
refrained from pointing this out to her sister, though.
Jackie would have shaken her head with one of those
affectionate, half pitying smiles of hers and immediately
told her sister that a job *was* a nine-to-five routine most
of the time, that mother luck rarely visited, that men
were just ordinary mortals with ordinary bad habits, so
join the reality club and stop living in a dream world.

She was still standing there, daydreaming about the
magical mystery tour of the manor which lay in store
for her, the daily pleasures of looking at the various
paintings and artefacts, when the huge front door swung
open and she was confronted by a sight that momen-
tarily took her breath away.

A man, tall, lean and cloaked in black, stood in front
of her, silhouetted against the inky blackness of early
evening. He looked as though he belonged to another
era, a more dangerous, less civilised one, and somewhere, the thought flashed through her head, there
should be a white stallion, stamping and snorting in the
bitter cold.

Then she blinked and realised that of course it was an
illusion, she was just being silly.

'Who are you?' she asked in a timid voice, nervously clutching her coat around her because the hall was suddenly freezing cold from the outside air.

'Who,' the man replied coldly, divesting himself of the black coat to reveal a less startling grey suit, perfectly tailored and, Claire noticed uncomfortably, dramatically emphasising the sort of body that didn't usually belong to men in suits, 'might I ask, are you?'

He slung the coat on to the mint-coloured *chaise-longue* just behind him and turned to face her, staring at her until a deep red flush slowly crawled up her cheeks.

She was not adept at social banter at the best of times, and right now she was feeling horribly uncomfortable and, she suspected, probably looking like a goldfish as well with her mouth half open and her eyes huge and wary.

'I'm here for the job,' she stammered in a small voice, and the man clicked his tongue impatiently.

'Job? What job?'

He began moving off towards one of the many sitting-rooms downstairs, expecting her to follow, which she did, even though it struck her that she still didn't know his name.

'Cleaner,' she called from behind him. 'I saw the advertisement in the newspaper and I applied for the post.'

He turned to face her, his eyes narrowed, and she shrank back. He really was the most alarming man she had ever met. There was something forbidding in the hard set of his features, despite the suggestion of warmth in the curve of his mouth. His hair was dark, almost black, and his eyes were a peculiar shade of green. Not hazel, not blue-green, but pure, undiluted green, and fringed by thick, black lashes.

Those green eyes were roving over her now, taking her in inch by lazy inch, and she felt a spark of anger ignite inside of her. She knew very well that this arrogant man was most probably the so-called master of the house, and she knew that, to him, a cleaner was probably the lowest of the low, but there was no reason why she had to endure the indignity of his stare.

So with a rare attempt at rebellion she stuck her hands on her hips and tried to think of something very cutting to say, master or no master.

'You don't look like a cleaner,' he informed her, moving across to one of the sofas and sitting down.

He didn't gesture to her to do likewise and she decided that if this was a deliberate ploy then it was a good one, because she felt exposed and nervous standing where she was, like someone forced to appear solo on stage in front of a bank of critics.

'I do apologise,' she said neutrally, though from the look of amusement that crossed his face he could read the sarcasm in her voice quite easily.

'How old are you? Fifteen? Sixteen? Does your mother know that you're running about applying for jobs when you should be at school?'

That really was the last straw. Mild-mannered she might be, but she suddenly saw red.

'I am not fifteen,' she snapped, her face crimson, 'nor am I sixteen. And my mother is fully aware that I'm running about applying for jobs. In fact, I suspect she sincerely hopes I get one, considering I'm twenty years old and I've just finished at art college!'

'In which case,' he said smoothly, 'why are you applying for a job as a cleaner? Are you hoping to bring something creative to the post? Perhaps redesign the dust into artistic swirls?'

Claire clenched her fists by her sides and looked away from him.

Very cool, she thought, very urbane to sit there and confuse me with lazy, sophisticated innuendoes. She hated men like that. Or at least, she thought honestly, she should do. But what she was feeling wasn't hatred. It was far from that. She felt uncomfortable, exposed, conscious of her womanhood in a way that she never had in her life before. It was a heady, exhilarating, scary feeling, like freefalling from a plane, and in a strange way it was addictive too. She didn't want him to stop looking at her. She had to force herself to come back down to Planet Earth.

'I need the money,' she said bluntly, 'and I like this house. Manor,' she corrected hastily. 'I like beautiful things, and this house—sorry, manor—is full of beautiful objects. I studied art at college, you see. Did I mention that to you? I've always loved paintings, sculptures; they're so much more *soothing* than all that grit and grime we see around us every day. Don't you think?'

He was nodding in an abstracted sort of way and she wondered whether she was on the verge of losing his attention. He was probably finding her gauche and earnest, but she wasn't the sort to play verbal games; she didn't know how.

'I'm sorry,' she said, taking refuge in as cool a tone of voice as she could muster, but feeling deflated. 'I'm afraid I don't know your name.'

'Forrester. James Forrester.' He didn't stretch out his hand to hers. Instead he joined his fingers under his chin and continued to survey her with the sort of frank appraisal which she decided bordered on rude. 'And your name is...?'

'Claire Harper.' That said, there didn't seem much else to say and she hovered indecisively, wondering whether she could find the self-possession to smile blankly, utter a few closing pleasantries and take her leave.

He made her nervous and she wondered whether the housekeeper, Mrs Evans, had been right when she'd said that he was not around very much.

'Why don't you sit down,' he said, 'you look like a frightened animal about to turn tail and take flight. I won't eat you.'

Ha ha, Claire thought, smiling weakly, very funny. She would have to get some lessons from her sister on how to deal with men like him. Jackie was far more adept when it came to the fine art of social interaction and *savoir-faire*. Staring and stammering definitely weren't top of the league when it came to masterful social interaction.

'I really can't,' she mumbled. 'I want to get back before it's too dark.'

'I don't think it's possible to get any darker, do you? How did you get here? I assume you didn't drive; there's no car in the courtyard. Did you cycle?'

Claire shook her head. 'Bus, then I walked the mile or so from the bus stop,' she confessed, and he stared at her as though the concept of walking was very far removed from his idea of ways and means of getting from A to B.

'Come on,' he said, standing up. 'I'll run you back in my car.'

She refused, of course, protested, backed away, which only brought a curl of amusement to his lips, but in the end he drove her back to her lodgings in his sleek burgundy convertible Mercedes, and when she hurriedly tripped out of the car, he followed her up to the house, putting her in a position whereby to stand at the door and tell him to go would have seemed impossibly childish.

'You live here?' he asked in amazement, looking around the kitchen, and she followed the direction of his gaze.

It was shabby. The linoleum was lifting from the floor, the appliances all looked as though they had seen better times in the Boer war and God only knew when the walls had last had a lick of paint. Judging from the accumulated layers of grime, decades ago. If you think this is bad, she wanted to tell him, you ought to see the bedrooms, but then she had a sudden, disturbing picture of him in her bedroom and launched into a confused apology for the scrappy condition of the kitchen, explaining how difficult it was to get somewhere cheap and presentable to rent when landlords seemed to adhere to the belief that there was no reason to do anything but the very basic with their accommodation when lack of choice would bring tenants anyway.

Her voice trailed off and she stared at him nervously. The other girls were not yet back from work, although they would be shortly, and in her haste to hurry him out of the house before they returned and began asking her a series of questions about him, she took him by the arm to lead him back to the side door.

The jolt of awareness that shot through her at the slight physical contact brought hectic colour to her cheeks and she sprang back, alarmed.

'Take good care of my house,' he drawled, watching her face and leaving her with the impression that he was well aware of the effect he had on her. 'Sorry—manor.'

There was a little silence and she raised her eyes reluctantly to his, and for some reason her head began to spin and her mouth went completely dry. He was so overpowering, with those potent, dark good looks and that air of lazy sex appeal which she could glimpse quite easily now that some of his cold arrogance was no longer in evidence.

Only when he left did she relax, leaning heavily against the door and breathlessly telling herself that Jackie would die laughing if she could see her now.

She would have seen all that crazy self-consciousness and stammering shyness as one hundred per cent predictable. If you'd read fewer books and done more partying as a girl, if Mum and Dad hadn't treated you like breakable china, if you'd stayed in London and allowed me to sort you out, if, if, if... Jackie would never have understood.

She didn't understand it herself. In the car, surrounded by darkness, listening to that deep, sexy voice as he chatted about Frilton Manor, she had felt as though she was drowning. Confused and nervous, but wonderfully so. As if she was truly alive for the first time in her life. Sleeping Beauty awakened by a magical kiss.

It was another fortnight before she saw him again, but after that they seemed to bump into each other on a regular basis. He was working from home. She gleaned that from Mrs Evans, who also told her that that in itself was highly unusual.

Unusual or not, Claire found that the prospect of him being in the manor made her wake up in the mornings raring to go, although she didn't question why this should be so. She found herself listening for his footsteps, contriving to be in the same room as he was, always making sure that there was a duster and a can of polish in her hand, of course. She was, she knew, beginning to feed off the illicit thrill of seeing his dark, handsome face, hearing the deep timbre of his voice. She was still looking in the newspapers for jobs, but half-heartedly, because a part of her didn't want to have to give up her job at Frilton Manor, or else continue at it on weekends only, when he wasn't guaranteed to be around.

She was about to leave one evening when he appeared from the direction of the library, which doubled as his office, and called out to her. She found herself immediately smiling at him, appreciatively taking in the casual green cords and thick off-white jumper. He could wear anything, she had decided, and still look unbearably, terrifyingly handsome.

He looked at her with that lazy amusement which she *knew* she had glimpsed in his eyes occasionally, and which always made her tremble with awareness, and then surprised her by asking her to join him for a drink.

'Or some coffee,' he said, 'if you don't drink.'

'Oh, I do!' she lied, blushing. 'I'd love a...' she thought quickly about it '...gin and tonic.'

It was after six and already pitch black outside with the threat of snow hanging in the air, and she knew that she should leave before the threat became reality, but the temptation to linger in his company was too irresistible.

She followed him into his study, where a carved mahogany bar blended comfortably with the rest of the furniture, and looked around her guilelessly while he poured her a drink.

It was a shame, she thought, that he had caught her like this at the end of the day, when she was looking a little worse for wear, but at least she was wearing her best-fitting pair of jeans and a navy blue baggy cotton jumper which she knew was flattering with her shade of eyes and dark hair.

He handed her the drink and gestured for her to sit down, while he perched on the edge of the desk, looking down at her from what seemed a great height.

She was beginning to feel nervous and jumpy, which always seemed to be the case whenever she got too close to him, when he broke the silence by asking her whether she had found a job as yet.

Claire looked at him, startled.

'No,' she stammered, frowning, 'I haven't. I'm sorry. They're terribly difficult to find, or at least the right ones are. Why do you ask? Do you want to get rid of me?' She hoped, as she stared at him, that she didn't look too pleading, but the thought of never seeing him again made her feel slightly sick.

He gave her a long, careful look. 'Of course not. I just imagined that working here can't exactly be riveting for a girl of your age. Not on a full-time basis, at any rate. It's a beautiful house, full of beautiful things, but the job isn't exactly the height of intellectual stimulation, is it? And I gather from the little I've seen of you that you're not an unintelligent girl.'

She wished that he would stop calling her a girl. She was a woman, not a ten-year-old in a gingham dress with her hair in pigtails. She was twenty years old, wasn't she? She had been to college, hadn't she? And she was sitting here now with a glass of gin and tonic in her hand, and that was a very adult drink indeed. She took a mouthful of it and tried to control the grimace of distaste from crossing her features.

'I enjoy working here,' she murmured evasively, carefully putting the glass on the table next to her and then sitting on her hands because they were showing a tendency to tremble.

'Why?'

'Why?' She looked at him blankly. 'Because...' Her voice trailed off while she tried to think of some logical reason to explain why a college graduate qualified to do a completely different job should be content with a cleaning job at Frilton Manor, however splendid a house it was.

'Because...?' he prompted, throwing his head back to swallow from his glass.

She watched him, fascinated by the strong, brown column of his throat, the long fingers, the forearm finely sprinkled with dark hair. She was still staring at him when his eyes met hers and she started guiltily.

'Because,' she said, trying to remember the question.

'Because, perhaps, it's a challenge?' he drawled. 'Come on, Claire, be honest with me. Is there some other reason for your working here?' His green eyes were sharp on her face. 'You seem honest enough, but who knows? Perhaps there's a boyfriend lurking on the sidelines somewhere, and the two of you are simply biding your time until you decide which bits of silver you're going to lift.'

She jumped to her feet angrily, her cheeks flaming red.

'How can you even think such a thing?' she asked fiercely. 'I wouldn't...I couldn't...there's no boyfriend lurking on the sidelines! I wouldn't dream of...' His implications were so staggering that she was finding it difficult to articulate, and she grabbed the glass from the table, swallowing the remainder of the drink in one long gulp. There was a rush of blood to her head and for a minute she thought that she was going to faint but she gritted her teeth together and looked at him straight in the eye.

'It was merely a passing thought,' he said, shrugging, 'and I'm surprised you can't understand my line of questioning. Why would a beautiful girl like you be willing to spend pretty much all day here,' he gestured around him, 'when there are far more exciting things happening in the big bad world outside?'

'I am not a girl!' she heard herself say in a loud voice, 'I'm a woman!' Had he called her beautiful? He had!

There was a long silence, during which she could hear her heart thumping in her chest, even if he couldn't. She hardly dared breathe and she had the funny feeling that he was looking at her in a completely different way. Or was it just the gin and tonic going to her head? Two glasses of cider and she felt tipsy. Perhaps after one gin and tonic she was beginning to hallucinate.

'Yes, I suppose you are,' he said blandly.

'But not like the sort of women that you're accustomed to, is that it? Is that what you're implying?'

'I didn't think that I was implying anything.'

'You haven't answered my question. Not the first bit of it, anyway.' These were not at all the things she wanted to say, she realised, but for some reason they were spilling out of her mouth of their own accord and the brain seemed to have very little say in the matter.

Standing up as she was, she was on an eye-to-eye level with him. He was within touching distance, she thought.

'All right,' he said as though the matter was really of no great importance to him anyway, 'if you really want to know, no, you're nothing like the sort of women that I'm accustomed to. In fact, I can't recall meeting anyone like you in a very long time. Are you usually so forthright?'

'I don't believe in playing games with people.'

'We shouldn't be having this conversation,' he said heavily, and it was on the tip of her tongue to ask him why not when it struck her precisely why not.

Here they were, alone, in a semi-lit room which carried its own seductive atmosphere of intimacy, having a conversation about what was basically sex. It was a dangerous situation, but it was also an exciting one, one in which Claire had never before found herself.

Her emotional life, at the age of twenty, was as pristine as the driven snow. She had had boyfriends, that was inevitable, but they had all been passing interests, not one of them serious enough to make her lose any sleep.

'I only wanted to find out a bit more about you,' she said weakly.

'About which aspect of my life in particular?' he asked with a return to his normal dry tone of voice, although something in his manner wasn't as relaxed as she knew he was trying to appear.

She looked at him vaguely and he said, raising his eyebrows in an amused question, 'The sexual aspect?'

'Sexual aspect?' The frankness of the question horrified and excited her at the same time. Was this how the upper echelons communicated all the time? It wasn't as if she didn't know about sex, but it was the thought of him in a sexual situation that addled her. It wasn't just that beneath those clothes it was easy to discern a physically powerful body. It was much more than that. It was his personality, the combination of ruthlessness and sensuality that made for such a heady mix.

She was certainly feeling very heady now. Doubtless the drink had something to do with it, but, she had to admit in all honesty, not really a great deal.

There was a thick silence, and then she said recklessly, 'All right, yes, I can't deny that I'm curious about the sexual aspect of your life. Have you slept with lots of women?'

'What do you think?'

Claire stared at him nervously. 'I don't know. I suppose you have. I mean, you're...'

'What?' he asked softly, and she bit down on her lower lip, wishing now that the conversation had never got started.

'Attractive, I guess.' Now that it was out, now that she had admitted that she was attracted to him, she began to feel considerably braver. Two months ago she would have run a mile at the thought of this type of conversation. She had always tended to shy away from anything that was provocative or blatant. It was a trait which her parents thought was charming, but which she personally considered an anachronism in this day and age when sexual liberation was so commonplace that it wasn't even discussed.

Right now, though, her emotions were calling the tune and her mouth just seemed to be dancing to its music, uttering things that she would never have imagined herself saying to a man in a million years.

'In fact, I'm very attracted to you,' she said boldly.

He was staring at her and the intensity of his gaze brought a rush of colour to her cheeks.

'That's very flattering,' he murmured, raking his fingers through his hair, 'but you'd be better off confining your infatuations to someone nearer your age.'

'Does that mean that you don't find me attractive?'

'You're putting words into my mouth.'

She knew that he would have stood up and walked away, probably out of the room if not out of the house, but she was standing directly in front of him, blocking an easy exit.

'I'm not attracted to boys nearer my age. They're immature. They don't do anything for me.' She was breathing quickly now and the palms of her hands were damp with perspiration.

'You don't know what you're saying,' he said roughly. 'That's the drink talking.'

'No, it's not!' She took the smallest of steps towards him and rested her hand against his neck, brushing it with her thumb.

His eyes darkened and she was pleased to see that he wasn't in total control either.

Does that mean that he's attracted to me? she wondered. He hadn't said otherwise, had he? And he *had* invited her to have a drink with him. That hadn't been necessary, had it? So what did that add up to? she wondered feverishly.

There seemed only one way to find out. With one impulsive movement she pressed her mouth against his, parting her lips to allow her questing tongue entry into his mouth, and with a groan he began kissing her, really kissing her.

It was like being lifted off her feet and transported into a completely new dimension. He raised his hands to cup her face, pulling her towards him, devouring her with a savagery which made her blood boil.

When he slipped his hand underneath her jumper to caress her breast through the shirt, she had an insane desire to rip her clothes off so that she could feel flesh against flesh. Her nipples were hard and aching and she begged in a high, pleading voice,

'Make love to me. I want you. I need you, I love you.'

She was so consumed by the ferocity of her own wanting that it took a few seconds to realise that he had frozen. She opened her eyes and looked at him in bewilderment.

'What is it?' she asked, reluctant to let go of the mood but knowing that she had no choice.

'What the hell do you think?' he grated, literally lifting her off her feet to move her aside. 'I think it's time that you left.'

'Why? What have I done?'

'There's no room in my life for an infatuated child,' he bit out grimly, and her eyes filled with tears. 'This is all my fault. I'm completely to blame,' he continued. 'I'm just glad that I came to my senses before I ended up doing something that I would have lived to regret.' He stood up and said dispassionately, 'You can stay in here a couple of minutes, enough time to come to your senses, and then I suggest you leave.'

'But you don't understand! I love you!'

'You don't know the meaning of the word,' he rasped harshly. 'And in view of what's happened here tonight, I think it might be a good idea if you didn't return.'

'No!'

She stared at him in mute silence and finally he said with a heavy sigh, 'All right. You can stay, but keep out of my way. I shall be here for the next week and I don't want to... Let's just say that I'm only a man.' He gave her a harsh, impatient look, then he was gone and she was left standing alone in the study and wondering what she would do now.

CHAPTER THREE

SHE couldn't leave. Thinking back about it, and God knew she had thought about it all a million times over the past few months, she could see that she should have done. She should have nipped her growing love for him in the bud, and then she might have been able to retreat from the relationship with her dignity and emotional stability relatively intact.

But she stayed, and for a while things settled down into an uneasy pattern. James was hardly around, and when he was she knew that he was avoiding her. The few times they bumped into each other, he was scrupulously polite to her, and she in turn tried to hide the lovesick longing in her eyes.

She still hadn't breathed a word of what was happening to either her parents, who would have been appalled by the whole thing, or to Jackie, who would have laughed and insisted that it was all a girlish crush, the result of having led such a retiring, introverted life as far as the opposite sex were concerned.

Then, the unthinkable happened. She went for an interview at a small but fast-expanding local advertising firm who were looking for someone to work in their creative department.

'I expect you won't have to give any notice at this cleaning job that you're doing,' her prospective boss said, reading through her application form and tapping his fingers on the desk as though he had more pressing things to do and really wanted the interview to conclude as quickly and painlessly as possible.

Claire looked at the downbent head miserably. She had already been shown around the company, met some of the people she would be working with, if she managed to land the job, and had been introduced to some of the types of work that she would be expected to do, and it was all exactly what she had had in mind when she had first moved to Reading from London.

So there was no way that she could blow her chances away by trying to juggle Frilton Manor and the job, and there was also no way that she could maintain any sort of part-time work at the Manor in the evenings because Tony, now looking at her impatiently and waiting for her answer, had told her from the start that overtime was unpaid and expected when the situation demanded, take it or leave it.

'Well?' he asked. He had a high, slightly effeminate voice and was good looking in a very blond, vaguely limpid way. He was her idea of what Adonis must have looked like. She had a suspicion that he probably never travelled without a comb in the breast pocket of his jacket and was addicted to looking at himself in mirrors. But she knew that all that concealed a fairly sharp brain because she had seen some examples of his work and they were brilliant.

'Yes. I mean no. I mean,' she said, gathering her thoughts together with effort, 'I won't have to give any notice. Perhaps a couple of days or so.'

'Good.' He looked at his watch and issued her with his first smile since she had arrived two hours ago. 'In that case, you can start next Monday. Eight-thirty sharp. Sandra will take care of you until you find your feet, and Personnel will send you your contract through the post later today. You should have it by tomorrow, or day after latest.'

Claire's mouth sagged open.

'I can see you're thrilled,' Tony said smugly. 'I needn't tell you that you were one of thirty who applied for the job. We had a much bigger response than we had expected.' He stood up and she followed suit hurriedly. 'I must dash now,' he said, moving or rather gliding towards the door and opening it for her. 'Meetings call.'

She was still in a daze by the time she made it to Frilton Manor and she spent the remainder of the day viciously dusting and cleaning. She was wiping the row of books in the study when the door opened and she turned around to see James standing framed in the doorway, looking at her as though she had taken leave of her senses.

They stared at each other in silence for a while then he moved towards the desk and said drily,

'You look murderous. I didn't think that dusting a few books could do that to anyone.' He began pressing buttons on the small computer on the desk, with his back to her, and she wondered whether he had forgotten about her being there at all.

'I've got a job,' she informed him bluntly, and he stopped what he was doing and turned around to face her.

It was obvious that he had just come from work, from the looks of it to continue working from the study. His jacket had been discarded, and the sleeves of his shirt were carelessly rolled back to the elbows, but he was still wearing his suit trousers, and his tie, deep burgundy silk, which had been tugged down so that the top button of his shirt could be undone. Did he know how devastatingly sexy he looked, standing there, watching her with those disconcerting green eyes?

'Congratulations,' he said politely. 'Well done. Where is it?'

She told him, taking a masochistic delight in dwelling on the attractive package that had been offered her, even though she knew that her voice sounded far removed from enthusiastic.

'I suppose you're relieved,' she finished, looking at him defiantly.

'Why should I be?'

'Because,' Claire continued relentlessly, 'you won't have to dodge my childish infatuation with you any longer.' What did she have to lose by saying all this? she asked herself fiercely. It made her feel good getting it all off her chest, anyway.

'Your childish infatuation was very flattering to an old man like myself,' he said with a grim smile. 'For the first time I began to understand why some older men can't resist the lure of a much younger woman.'

Ah. He had called her a woman. That felt good. She stood with her hands behind her back and lifted her chin.

'You act as though you're a hundred. How old are you?'

'Do you have to be so outspoken?' he asked with the ghost of a smile.

'You know it's the way I am,' Claire said very coolly, considering her throat felt like sandpaper.

'I'm thirty-four.'

'Is that all?'

'You mean I look older?' He laughed. 'Watch it, I might start getting a complex.'

This was the first time since their uneasy pact of silence that they were speaking to each other without reservation, and she felt herself relax and open up. He was the only man she had ever met who could do that to her, make her feel confident enough to speak her mind without thinking too much about the consequences.

'I mean,' she explained, 'that's awfully young to own all this.' She made a broad sweeping gesture. 'Did you inherit it?'

'Not exactly. Would you like a drink? Anything but gin and tonic.'

Claire shook her head, blushing at the glint that flitted through his eyes when he said that.

He turned and poured himself a drink from the bar and continued talking. 'My uncle owned all this, and I suppose I had always loved the place ever since I had been a child. I expect I would have inherited it in due course—he was childless—but eight years ago he ran into some financial problems, coincidentally at a time when business was booming for me and I bought him out.' He faced her and she could see pride in his expression when he looked around the room.

'Where does he live now?'

'He died two years ago,' James said abruptly. 'Penniless. It transpired that, over the course of time, he had gambled away a considerable amount of money.'

'That's too bad,' Claire offered sympathetically, but it was beyond her comprehension how anyone could gamble away their money. She had spent a lifetime guided by parents who carefully conserved theirs, spending on essentials and saving up for the little luxuries. It was a trait which she, and Jackie to some extent, had inherited.

'And what about you?' he asked, watching her from under his lashes. 'Are you as guileless as you seem or are there any skeletons in your closet?'

Skeletons? The thought was ludicrous. She smiled and chatted away happily about her parents, her sister, her childhood, and it was only when she happened to glance at her watch that she saw how much time had elapsed. If she didn't hurry, she would miss her bus and then there would be another forty-minute wait for the next one, if indeed it had the decency to arrive on time, which was by no means guaranteed.

She laughed apologetically for her rambling reminiscences and said, tripping over her words, 'I must go. I've bored you, I suppose, but once I start talking about my family I tend to get a bit carried away. I really came to tell you that as from Monday you'll have to find someone else to clean.'

'And what a pity that's going to be,' he said, looking at her steadily until her head began to throb.

The atmosphere became thicker and when he stepped towards her, she could feel every nerve in her body begin to go haywire.

'You know I don't want to go,' she muttered breathlessly. 'You know why. What I feel for you isn't infatuation, I really am in love with you. I know it's sudden, but I know my mind.' Now, she thought, he's going to send me on my way, and since I don't want to go, I should have held my tongue and not said anything. But he didn't say a word. Not at first, at any rate.

He only spoke when he was standing close to her.

'I'm not looking for love.'

It wasn't what she had been expecting to hear. She had expected to see that shutter clamp down over his eyes, the way it had the first time she had told him how she felt, had expected his impatient dismissal.

'No?' she said as nervously as if he was touching her, when in fact his hands were in his pockets.

'Love complicates things,' he continued in that same, flat voice, 'and I don't want my life to be complicated.

I want you—something about you turns me on, maybe that openness of yours is more dangerous than I originally thought—but I don't need a woman who's going to be cloying afterwards.'

'No,' Claire repeated obediently, even though she was too mesmerised by him to take in much of what he was saying.

'I've done my damndest to fight this thing, this attraction I feel for you, but, as you say, you're no longer a child.'

'Yes,' she contributed helpfully. What happens now? she wondered. Throwing herself at him had been easy, she had acted purely on instinct, but the way he was laying out the terms and conditions of his seduction confused her, even though, looking at him, she wanted him more than anything or anyone in her entire life.

'If I'm scaring you off,' he said abruptly, 'please leave.'

'You're not scaring me off,' she whispered timidly, venturing a smile, and placing a hand on the top button of her blouse. Did he want her to undress here? Was this how it would be done?

He pulled her hand away and smiled, and it altered the contours of his face completely. She wasn't intimidated now. She let him take her up to his bedroom and when he shut the door behind him she only felt excited and a little frightened at the same time.

She had never been up to his bedroom before. Mrs Evans cleaned certain rooms in the house and this was one of them, so she stared around her in open curiosity.

It was very large, large enough to accommodate an entire three-piece suite at one end, while at the other was a massive desk, with yet another computer terminal on it, as well as a telephone, uncomfortably modern amid the lush, potent eighteenth-century atmosphere of everything else.

The wardrobes lining the room were out of deep wood, richly polished and gleaming, and the king-size bed was in colours of burnished reds. It was a man's room, without any of the softening touches a woman would not have been able to resist. But then why should there be any feminine touches, she thought, when he had already told her that he didn't care for women cluttering up his life?

She looked at him wordlessly and he said under his breath, 'Relax. You look as though you're preparing yourself to face the Chinese Water Torture.'

That made her laugh and he said approvingly, 'That's better.'

'I've never...' Claire began awkwardly. 'You're the first...'

'That's good,' he murmured huskily, loosening his tie to toss it across on a chair, followed by his shirt.

She placed the palms of her hands on his chest and gave a sharp intake of breath. After all this time nurturing her dreams, it was almost unbearable to feel his skin against hers like this.

'You don't know how exquisite you are,' he said, cupping her face with his hands. 'Those big blue eyes, that look of innocence. I feel like the big bad wolf.' He smiled and she looked up at him shyly.

'Don't. I wouldn't want anyone else to make love to me.' She almost said because she loved him so much, but then she remembered what he had told her, and she bit back the words.

'Unzip my trousers,' he told her and she raised trembling hands to the waistband, not daring to look at what she was doing. She had never seen a naked man before and the thought of seeing him now, without any clothes on, was scaring her half to death, even though she knew that he was taking his time with her, being very gentle.

She could feel his arousal pushing against the zip, though, and she unsteadily pushed the trousers down, watching as he stepped out of them, his eyes never leaving her face.

Then he began to undress her, kissing her at the same time, his mouth lingering over hers while his fingers brushed aside the flimsy barrier of her clothes.

He lifted her and carried her to the bed, then he said seriously, 'There's still time to change your mind. I won't do anything you don't want me to.'

'I want you, James Forrester,' she said honestly, 'I'm not going to change my mind about that. Ever.'

'Nothing in life is permanent, remember that,' he said shortly, and she wished that she hadn't said it, but he wasn't about to enlarge on his comment. He placed light little kisses on her neck, then, as if he could no longer restrain himself, his mouth covered hers in an urgent kiss that barely gave her room to breathe.

He stripped himself of the final barrier of his clothing and she felt him hard against her thigh, and the sensation sent a shudder running through her. Tentatively she ran her hands along his back, tracing the taut, corded muscles of his shoulders, and he bent his head to nuzzle against her breasts until she could no longer stand it and pressed his head over one aching tip, groaning as he took it into his mouth and suckled hard on it.

He was letting her set the pace, controlling himself so that she could dictate when she was ready for their love-making to progress one stage further.

He caressed the smooth lines of her body, running his hand quickly and expertly along her side and thigh, and she parted her legs for him so that he could cup the moistness between them, gradually exploring her until she cried out in frustrated longing.

She had felt inhibited to start with, she had wondered whether, for all her love and hunger for him, she would feel the requisite need, or whatever it was she should feel, when he began to make love to her.

Now, with each electrifying caress making her body melt, she urged him on to bring her to the final peak. As she felt him move inside her, her body tensed fractionally, then he began thrusting slowly and gently, building up more momentum as she relaxed, and finally moving aggressively against her, taking her to an explosive climax.

All this time later, Claire could still remember vividly how she felt that very first time, a mixture of wonder and desire and bottomless love, although she was already learning quickly to keep those thoughts to herself.

'We didn't take any precautions,' he said, facing her. 'I don't suppose that you're on . . .'

'No, I'm not,' Claire said quickly.

'I don't want you getting pregnant, and I shouldn't imagine that you would want it either.'

'No, of course not,' she said, meaning I can't think of anything nicer than having your babies, but knowing that to express anything of that nature was out of the question.

'You're young,' he said heavily, 'you have your whole life ahead of you, and as for me, let's just say that I want an heir to the "throne" even less than I want a woman with whom to share it.' He looked at her when he said this and Claire tried to school her features into an expressionless mask because she knew what he was

doing. It was what he had done from the very beginning, warned her off him.

'Why are you so bitter?' she asked, looking into the
green eyes.

'Is that how I sound?' He appeared to give the matter
some thought. 'I suppose it is. The fact is that experience teaches you a lot of lessons, and the first lesson
is that it's a mistake to be too trusting.'

'Were you? Too trusting, that is?' She reached out to
stroke his face and he caught her hand in his.

'The second valuable lesson,' he said, ignoring her
question, 'is that curiosity killed the cat.'

'Meaning that you don't want me asking any questions about your private life.'

'That's right.'

'But I want to know you! I want to find out about
you.' The words were out before she could stop them
and she saw the expression on his face become closed
and terse. How could he change so quickly? she wondered. One minute he was tenderness itself, the next it
was as though she was staring at a stranger and one who
was adamantly going to remain that way.

'And I don't need a woman clinging on to me, Claire,
trying to understand me. You're an attractive girl, but
you're not that attractive.'

She felt tears spring to her eyes at this and she looked
away quickly. At least, she tried to console herself, he
was being honest, at least he wasn't giving her some airy-
fairy story about everlasting love just because he wanted
to have a fling with her. She supposed she ought to be
grateful for that.

'You certainly have a way with words,' she said unsteadily, and the lazy smile returned to his face.

'So do you.' He kissed her and she closed her eyes, losing herself in a renewed surge of passion.

If what he wanted was an affair with no strings attached, then that was what she would give him. Love, she thought, did funny things to a person. It makes them blind to the consequences of a relationship. She would never have dreamt that she would find herself in the position of mistress, accepting the rules of someone else's game. She had always imagined that when she fell in love, it would be reciprocated, that all that romantic bliss which she had yearned for would be returned. She had watched her sister from the sidelines, bringing home her boyfriends, breaking up with them, falling in and out of love, and she had made up her mind that she would never fall victim to that. Love, for her, would be a grand affair of the heart. Everything in her life had conspired in those childhood dreams. Her sister's temperament, bold, outspoken, extrovert, had inadvertently moulded her own shy girlishness, and, pampered and protected by parents who only had watchful eyes for her more streetwise sister, she had been left ample room to build her castles and knights. How was she ever to guess that this mad desire, this foolish love, would be painful and, worse, one-way?

She also never knew that it would have the power to hold her in its grip even though, time and time again, common sense told her to pack her bags and run.

In retrospect, she wondered whether she had ever had any choice in the matter, or whether the sheer power of her emotions had had her at its mercy from the very first minute she clapped eyes on him.

Deep inside, there was still a ray of hope that one day he would turn around and tell her that he loved her, that she had somehow managed to break through that barrier of his which stood between them like an invisible shield, however desperately she tried to break it down.

In the beginning, she had had all the confidence of youth, the glorious belief that her love would win the day, that in the end he just wouldn't be able to resist the devotion she was so eager to shower on him. She had never been in love before, and the compulsion to be with him, the ecstasy when she was with him, swept her into a strange, timeless orbit where normal thought processes and common sense had no place. And he wanted her. That was something that never failed to thrill her, but when she asked him about it, hoping to elicit the responses she wanted to hear, he only ever smiled and looked at her as though she would know the answer to her question if she looked hard enough.

She didn't know the answer, though, and she could remember looking at him after that first time that they had made love, not really caring one way or another. She had been living on a day-to-day basis, prey to her emotions for the first time in her life, and quite happy to flow with the tide.

She could remember wishing that he would show more emotion at the thought of her no longer working for him, though.

'Will you miss me?' she had asked, arching up to nuzzle her chin against his cheek, which was rough with darkened stubble. She had felt wildly romantic. She was so in love, what more could she have asked than for this dark, powerful, utterly devastating man to have taken her virginity?

He looked genuinely perplexed at that question. He raised his eyebrows and said, 'Why on earth should I?'

'I shall miss you,' Claire said with a smile. 'I'll miss everything about you. The way you look, the way you speak, the things you say...'

He looked at her as though torn between irritation at this admission, and satisfaction.

'I'd rather,' he said at last, 'you kept your words of endearment to yourself.'

'Why?' Her brow cleared. 'You mean because you don't want to have to keep reminding me that this is a relationship with no strings attached?'

He shrugged, his mind wandering as he turned his attention to her body. He had a way of looking at her that made her want to be uninhibited. There was almost a physical sexual pleasure to be derived from the way his eyes lingered over every inch of her. Just being the object of his lazy observation was more potent an aphrodisiac than anything she could imagine.

'I always like to make it clear to the women I...date...that I'm not on the look-out for a prospective wife.'

'Is that supposed to turn me on?' she asked, and he raised his eyes to hers. There was a proprietorial flare in them that made her giddy with want.

'Everything about me turns you on,' he murmured, tugging at her lower lip with his teeth. 'Haven't you already told me so?'

'You're very modest!'

'I know.'

'Is that,' she couldn't help asking, 'what women see in you?'

'Maybe,' he said, and there was a touch of coolness in his voice now. 'Or maybe it's the size of the bank balance.' He looked at her and she met his gaze steadily.

'I soon make it clear that this particular bank balance isn't up for grabs, though.'

'How straightforward,' Claire murmured, refusing to let that remark niggle away at her. All right, so he insisted on warning her off. Didn't he know that it was too late, that she had already taken the bait? She stroked his broad shoulders, then kissed his neck, her tongue flicking catlike along down to his chest, then back to his mouth. She felt wanton, and it was such a novel experience for her that she couldn't get enough of it.

'You still haven't told me whether you'll miss me,' she murmured huskily. 'You've issued dire warnings, informed me in no uncertain terms that I'm only here on a temporary basis, but the question is, will you miss me when I've gone?'

'You're a persistent little creature, aren't you?' he said with a slow smile. 'As to missing you, I might have if it weren't for the fact that I know you belong to me.'

A man accustomed to having what he wants. The thought flashed through her head, but she didn't feel the slightest twinge of alarm at that. She was too busy relishing the idea of being wanted by him in the first place.

'Does that mean that we'll continue to see each other?'

'Why not? And no bus trips to facilitate it either. I want you to use the cottage in the grounds. I don't know why I didn't think of that sooner. That flat of yours is a dump.'

'I could move out, go somewhere better. Somewhere more...'

'Hygienic?' he contributed. 'What makes you think that you'll be able to find anything better?'

'Because,' she explained, 'I've got a job now. I'll be able to afford more.'

'What? A flat?'

'Probably not,' she admitted. 'But I'd be able to rent a better room in a better house in a better location.'

'There is no better location for you than the cottage,' he said easily. 'That way all I have to do is reach out and have you.'

That should have made her angry, and from anyone else it would have, but all she felt was a thrill of desire. His warm hand cupped her breast, massaging it slowly, languorously, and she half closed her eyes with pleasure.

'I can't stay there,' she said unsteadily and his hand stilled.

'Why not?'

'Because I'd feel like a kept woman.'

'I want you, Claire. This warm, willing body of yours drives me to distraction. It's quite unlike anything I've ever experienced before, and I want to have you close by. I don't want to have to make love to you in silence, in a house where other people are around, listening.'

'Then at least let me pay rent,' she said quickly, and he glanced at her with a smile, as though the thought amused him. He named a nominal, ridiculous figure and she protested, at which his look of amusement grew.

'I don't need the money,' he said smoothly and she frowned.

'That's not the point. This has nothing to do with whether you need the money or not. It has to do with...'

'Pride?'

'Something like that.'

'How charming,' he drawled. 'And I thought that pride was an outdated commodity. Sometimes your ingenuousness is just a little too good to be true.'

Claire looked at him, bewildered. Underlying everything he said there was always a thread of cynicism that confused and intrigued her at the same time. He could be warm and direct and open, but she always felt that there was something else, something altogether more complex and enigmatic just beneath the surface.

'What do you mean?'

'I have yet to meet a woman who has refused my generosity on the grounds of pride. I'll be very interested to see how long this endearing naïveté lasts with you.'

That made her wince, but instead of apologising he laughed under his breath at her reaction.

I amuse him, she thought, I'm a curiosity, a species of female that he hasn't chanced upon for so long that he's forgotten we exist.

In the months to come, she wondered whether she shouldn't have left him the day that realisation dawned on her. She kept fooling herself, though, that she was still in control of the situation, even though she was so madly in love with him that she would have done anything to remain a part of his world. It was ironic, she sometimes thought, that after a lifetime starved of any sort of relationship that meant anything to her she should hurl herself without caution into the arms of a man who had nothing to offer. It was as if she had lived her life in a stoppered bottle and now she had become a slave to the man who had freed her. Aladdin and the lamp.

She moved into the cottage with a mixture of sheer pleasure at no longer being in the house which she had come to detest, and a certain apprehension which James swept aside with a wave of his hand when she mentioned it to him.

'It's superior here, isn't it?' he asked, and she nodded. 'Convenient?' Another nod, because she had bought herself a bicycle and was no longer relying on public transport. 'Could you have possibly got anything as pleasant for that sum of money?'

'Do you want more rent?' she asked anxiously, and he threw her one of those indulgent smiles which she was coming to recognise. He didn't bother to answer her question. Instead, he said, still smiling,

'So what's the problem?'

Put like that, she wondered whether she wasn't being over-sensitive. It wasn't as if she was unemployed and dependent on him totally for her upkeep. Anyway, she did pay him rent, scrupulously so, and she never accepted any presents from him. He had already made it clear what he thought of gold-diggers, a silent threat that she had better not be harbouring any ideas in that direction, and although he could not have been further from the truth if he'd tried, she saw no point in raising any doubts in his mind by accepting gifts from him.

That was no hardship, anyway. It was not in her nature to take what was offered for free, not unless she felt that she could repay the offering in her own way. In the past, when boys had taken her out for meals, albeit cheap and cheerful ones, she always reciprocated by returning the favour at a later date.

Her sister, already disapproving of their relationship, saw Claire's move to the cottage as a final piece of lunacy.

'You're not thinking straight,' she said bluntly. 'All that country air's gone to your head and turned you into a complete idiot.'

'Reading isn't "the country",' Claire responded, to which her sister snorted in disgust and accused her of trying to change the subject.

'You need to return to London,' she said imperiously, at which Claire smiled down the telephone because she could just imagine her sister's expression as she uttered that commanding bit of advice. 'You need to get a bit of civilisation back into your bones.'

Jackie adored giving orders. She had always been the more assertive of the two of them, and Claire had usually found herself giving way to her, but this time things were different. This time Jackie's opponent was far stronger, far more persuasive than she was.

'London isn't civilised,' Claire responded, to which there was another disgusted snort. As far as Jackie was concerned, to turn your back on London was something close to sheer madness. She had been born and bred in the country and she had been dying to leave it behind ever since she was a young girl. She couldn't understand why Claire could not appreciate what it had to offer.

'*That man* isn't civilised,' Jackie said bitingly, 'not from what you've told me at any rate. And if you didn't agree with me deep down, you would have been showing him off to everyone like mad. Move back up here,' she pleaded. 'I know heaps of people. I could introduce you to someone you'd like. Someone on whom you wouldn't be throwing your life away.'

That had been the tenor of her sister's criticisms ever since Claire had first told her about James. She needed to wake up, Jackie had decided, snap out of her pointless infatuation, find someone of her own ilk.

The thought of that made Claire shudder and she hurriedly wound up the conversation before her sister decided to fix a date for this introduction.

But the seeds of unease which had already been sown were now being watered.

She should have broken away, but wasn't it always so easy to see what should have been done in hindsight? How could she have broken away when he was in her bloodstream, an addictive, compelling sickness that could elevate her to those soaring heights where no one else could ever take her?

CHAPTER FOUR

'I'VE decided to come up and pay you a visit.'

Claire heard her sister's voice boom down the line and she automatically glanced around to make sure that Tony was not within hearing distance. He was in a foul temper and on the hunt for someone on whom he could vent it, and she was in no mood to be anybody's scapegoat.

She had not slept at all the night before, her eyes were burning, her head was hurting, and every time her wayward thoughts decided to wander off in the direction of James, she had an awful feeling that she was on the verge of breaking down completely. She would happily have taken the day off work. In fact she would happily have taken the rest of her life off work, told Tony that she was just retiring to somewhere very far away to die, but that would have been a final act of cowardice and she had spent too long being a coward, hiding from reality, pretending that things could change if she was patient enough.

Finding that photograph had catapulted her into making a decision about her relationship. It hadn't been easy. For a start, she wasn't used to making decisions, least of all decisions about her love-life. She had never been obliged to. She had never before found herself in a situation of having to relinquish someone who had become a part of her life, and now that she had walked away from James she had to keep reminding herself that it was for the best. It helped when she managed to shove the desolation to one side and convince herself that leaving him had freed her to continue with her life. She had spent the last few months on hold, in a state of limbo, and when she looked at it from that angle, she could almost feel exhilarated. Almost, but never completely, because lurking beneath all her persuasive arguments was the vision of a dismal, empty life without him.

Not that she allowed that to prey on her mind. She couldn't afford to. She needed strength, and she knew that she would find it because she had to, and it was in human nature to survive.

She still felt raw inside, though, but there wasn't much chance of Jackie understanding that and leaving her in peace. Sensitivity was not one of her sister's strong points, however caring she was. She had a tendency to steamroller her way over objections if she thought that she was in the right and there was no question that on the subject of James Jackie definitely considered herself to be on a winner.

'There's no need,' Claire said, eyeing the glass partition of Tony's office.

'There's every need. This thing, affair, call it what you will, has gone on for far too long...'

'You sound like Mum on one of her soap-boxes...'

'Don't interrupt. Where was I? Oh, yes—for *far too long*. You're such a ditherer, Claire. I shall zoom up there and sort everything out for you. It'll only take me forty minutes on the motorway. I can be with you by seven tonight.'

'I told you, there's no need. I've packed him in.' Not bad, she thought, the voice was light and at first glance could even pass for sounding nonchalant, as though packing men in was a hobby that she practised with regularity. She propped her head in her hands and blinked rapidly.

'You've done *what*?'

'Packed him in, Jackie,' she responded. 'Told him it's over, given him the big elbow...'

'I get the message,' Jackie said, sounding subdued. 'I still can't believe my ears, but I get the message.'

'Aren't you going to congratulate me?' Claire asked with a touch of bitterness. 'After all, it's what you've been advocating for months, isn't it?'

'Yes, but...'

'You've informed me often enough that the whole thing was destined to failure, that I was mad, stupid, naïve, childish, what were the other adjectives?'

'Was I wrong?' Jackie asked quietly, with concern in her voice. 'I only did it because I love you.'

'I know.' Claire sighed, a desperate little sound which she camouflaged under a dry laugh. 'You were right all along, of course. Though, to be fair, he never tried to kid me into believing that there was anything in our relationship. Ships that pass in the night, that's what we were.' This time the laugh was a little on the hysterical side and she had to fight down the urge to be sick. 'What he omitted to tell me was that he was married.'

There was a shocked gasp down the line and Claire began explaining about Olivia, not that she knew much, she realised in the telling. He had been married to a woman called Olivia. That was about it because he had thrown her only the barest of bones, and even those had been thrown under duress. What had she been like? How did she die? The questions had drummed on and on in her head for hours the night before. It was tempting to speculate on their relationship but every time she found herself doing that, she became even more depressed because he had obviously loved her madly and his love had been severed prematurely. That sort of situation, she realised, was insurmountable, because as far as he was concerned no one would ever be able to match up against a woman who had never had the time to expose her faults. She had died in full bloom and, next to her, how could any living, breathing woman measure up?

She didn't tell any of this to Jackie, though, but she knew that her sister was making exactly the same deductions. How could she fail to? You didn't have to be Sherlock Holmes to work out why James Forrester was not going to become involved in another relationship with a woman. He might sleep with them, share the more superficial aspects of his life with them, but that was about it. No doubt, if he ever married, it would be along the lines of a business arrangement, something that was beneficial to him and took no toll emotionally.

Jackie, now that the shock had dissipated, was musing aloud about this unexpected revelation. What more did he say? she kept pressing. Did he break down? That one was so amusing that for the first time that day Claire smiled. James Forrester, break down? What a laugh. He had probably possessed his reserves of self-control from the cradle.

Out of the corner of her eye, she saw Tony sauntering out of the office and she hurriedly cut short her sister's questions, but not before he had seen her surreptitiously replace the receiver. He strolled over and Claire looked at him cautiously. The girls on either side of her were pretending to work, but she knew that they were all ears, waiting for an explosion.

'Personal call?' he asked sarcastically. 'I don't suppose you'll have completed the design work on that after-shave advert, but you've got time for personal calls.

Amazing.' He gave her a reptilian smile and a few days ago that would have been enough to have ensured a mumbled apology and a red face, but Claire was at the end of her emotional tether. She returned his smile with a cool expression and informed him that that particular job had been completed.

Tony was pleasant most of the time, but when he wasn't he could be impossibly dictatorial, and right now she felt as though she had had enough of being dictated to.

'Has it really?' he said, looking taken aback, and she pulled out the sheets of board from her drawer, handing them to him.

'It has, really.' Claire smiled politely and he looked as though he would have liked to have said more, but he walked away, muttering and flicking through the boards, while Karen and Anne on either side of her stifled their giggles.

'What's got into you?' Karen asked, still grinning, though her eyes betrayed a certain amount of curiosity. 'You've never answered Tony back before. He looked as though you'd socked him in the jaw just then.'

'Don't tell me the worm has turned,' Anne murmured, smiling affectionately at Claire. Ever since she had first joined the company, Karen and Anne had taken it upon themselves to shelter Claire under their wing. They had come to the mutual decision that she lacked any kind of hard edge and would most probably break like a piece of china if she wasn't treated gently.

'That's one way of putting it,' Claire said grimly, and Karen frowned.

'You can't change!' she whispered. 'You're the eternal optimist. Especially compared to this little lot here.' She glanced theatrically around and Claire grinned.

'I've grown up,' she said seriously, realising that she meant it. She felt years older and centuries wiser, and with the realisation came a feeling of power that she would be able to carry on.

'In the space of twenty-four hours?'

'Something like that.'

'Enough chat!' Tony shouted from across the room, and Claire turned to him and said with a cool self-confidence which she never knew she possessed,

'We're still managing to work. Five minutes of conversation while we do our layouts isn't going to harm anyone.'

This time the silence in the room was complete. For a moment, Claire thought, Oh, help, I've gone too far, but then Tony smiled and shrugged his shoulders elegantly.

'What can I say to that piece of logic?' He was as volatile as summer weather, quick to thunder but then sunny again once the mood had passed. He disappeared back into his office and Karen gave her an enthusiastic thumbs-up sign.

One little triumph in the great tapestry of life, she thought, carrying on with her work, her hands on auto-drive as she sketched a series of layouts, while her mind was busy gnawing away at the issue of James.

She would have to leave the cottage, of course. It had always been a perk of the relationship, and the thought of continuing to live beneath his shadow, even if he did allow her to stay on, was out of the question.

By the time five-thirty rolled around, Claire knew exactly what her plan of action would be. She would go to the cottage and collect all her things, which should take all of five minutes since she had relatively little there and nothing bulky at all, then she would cycle up to the manor and give the keys to the housekeeper. James would not be around. He rarely made it back to the manor before eight at night and quite often not at all, preferring to stay at his London flat if he had meetings that ran on into the evening.

She practically flew back to the cottage, feeling like an intruder as she quickly began throwing her things into cases, starting with the bedroom and then gradually working her way downwards to the kitchen, where she scrupulously cleared away every single bottle of spice on the racks. Every single one brought back memories of meals she had cooked for him, even though to start with he had tried to discourage her from that little show of domesticity.

God, she thought, hurling them into her suitcase, how irritated he must have been at the thought of my cooking for him. Maybe he had suspected it as some kind of nest-building ploy.

It was ten-thirty by the time she had finished clearing out the cottage and had stacked the boxes neatly by the front door. She would have to return for them at a later date, when she had found somewhere permanent to live. In the meantime, she would be moving in with Karen, her friend from work, who lived a matter of minutes away from the office. It had been a spur-of-the-moment thought and Karen, bursting with curiosity but too kind to ask any outright questions, had agreed readily.

'It won't be anything like where you're accustomed to,' she had apologised, and Claire had smiled wryly, commenting that no, it would be much better, to which Karen had looked puzzled. She knew precious little about Claire, even though they saw each other socially at least once a week, usually for a quick bite in the town centre.

She had been back to the cottage a couple of times, though, and had been open-mouthed with awe.

With good reason, Claire thought, looking around her and fighting back the sadness. Every corner, every nook and cranny, held a memory and it amazed her to think just how much a part of her life he had become. It was as if she had never existed before she met him.

She cycled up to the manor, making sure that she kept to the side of the tree-lined avenue, certain that his car would be parked outside, in which case she would cycle off, but it wasn't and she breathed a sigh of relief as she raced up to the front door and rang the doorbell.

She could easily have waited until the following day to return the keys, but she wanted them out of her hands now, immediately. She felt as though she had done what she had to do and the sooner she rid herself of the things that reminded her of him, the sooner she could embark upon her recuperation.

She gave three more impatient little presses on the doorbell, tapping her foot and looking down at her watch. She didn't like cycling at this hour of the night, especially since it would take her at least half an hour of hectic pedalling to get back to Karen's place. Where the hell was Mrs Evans? She was about to give one final, very long, extremely irritated buzz when the door was pulled open and she found herself staring up at James. She closed her mouth but she couldn't wipe the look of shock from her face.

He was casually dressed, in a pair of black cords and a thick off-white jumper, the sleeves of which were shoved up to the elbows. He had stuck his hands in his pockets and he was staring down at her.

'What are you doing here?' she finally said when she had found her voice.

'I live here,' he said, giving her a long, amused smile, and she had a wild urge to knock his front teeth out. He must have a very short memory, she thought, to have forgotten what had happened between them the day before. He was certainly acting as though nothing between them had changed.

'That's not what I mean!' she began angrily, and he cut in, turning around and walking off,

'You'll freeze to death out there.' He glanced over his shoulder, his hands still in his pockets. 'Shut the door behind you. And they call this spring?'

He was heading off in the direction of the downstairs lounge and she dumped her bicycle down and stormed into the house, slamming the door behind her and hoping that she had broken a few window-panes in the process.

He had vanished into the lounge and she entered hard on his heels, panting a bit and red with anger, to find him pouring himself a drink.

'Care for something to drink?' he asked, facing her, and she glared back at him.

'No, I would not,' she bit out, enunciating her words very carefully, 'care for something to drink.'

'Are you sure?' he asked in a solicitous voice. 'You look as though you could do with one. All that exercise on that bicycle of yours. Quite bad for you, of course, as I've told you a dozen times. God knows why you don't get yourself a car.'

'Because I don't have the money!' she said, distracted and annoyed. 'And I didn't come here to chat about my mode of transport!'

He swallowed some of his drink, eyeing her over the rim of the glass.

'I came,' she said, 'to return this.' She held up the key, dangling it from its piece of string, and he looked at it, all amusement vanished from his face.

'You're being ridiculous, Claire,' he said, walking over to where she was standing on very unsteady legs, and relieving her of the key, which he tossed on to one of the small tables dotted about the room. 'I suppose this is a follow-on from yesterday?'

'Yes,' Claire responded tersely.

He looked at her, his green eyes dark with annoyance. 'For God's sake, aren't you being a bit childish?'

That made her see red. Childish? Her? Simply because she had decided to leave him? She might have guessed that this would have been his reaction, once his fury over her finding that photograph had subsided. She might have guessed that he would have simply expected her to carry on with him because, of course, no woman walked out on James Forrester. He was always the one who did the walking off.

'Yes,' she agreed, 'I'm being a bit childish. How clever you are to see through me like that.'

Her remark was like waving a red rag at the bull. He looked as though he wanted to throttle her.

'I thought we'd been through all that. I admit that I was damned angry when you showed me that photograph of Olivia, and maybe I over-reacted, but,' he shrugged, 'I expect that you would have found out about my marriage sooner or later.' His jaw tightened as he said that and she could see that the mere mention of his wife's name was enough to stir something in him, something that *she* had never been able to stir.

'Would I?' Claire replied coolly. 'Why? Would you have mentioned it to me?'

'Possibly not,' he admitted, swallowing the last of his drink and prowling restlessly around the room. 'But now that it's out in the open, I don't see why it should have any bearing on us.'

Claire looked at him in appalled amazement. 'I can't believe I'm hearing this,' she said incredulously. 'I find out, by accident, that you've been married, and you don't see why that should have any bearing on our relationship?'

'That's right.'

'You were secretive! You deliberately hid it from me! I feel as though I never knew you at all, as though I've spent months in bed with a complete stranger.'

'You're being over-dramatic.'

'And stop treating me like a halfwit!' she shouted, dogging his steps with her hands on her hips. 'I am not *being dramatic*!'

He stopped abruptly and she nearly crashed into him.

'Yes, you damn well are being dramatic. I wasn't secretive; as I said, I just didn't see the necessity of giving you an elaborate account of my past. But,' he added scathingly, 'with typical female logic, you find that impossible to accept, don't you? You'd not only like a blow-by-blow account of my marriage, no doubt you'd like a detailed post-mortem as well.'

'I would just have appreciated some honesty!'

'I thought I had given you quite a bit of that. I was honest enough when I told you that I didn't want commitment, and I thought that you accepted that.'

'I did.'

'Then where's the problem?' His brows were drawn together, giving his face a harsh arrogant stamp, and she realised that he was controlling his temper but only just.

'The problem is that I'm not prepared to live in someone else's shadow.'

'What exactly are you saying, Claire?' he asked in a soft, forbidding voice, his green eyes hard as he stared at her. 'That you were looking for some kind of commitment with me even though I told you I wasn't interested?'

'I suppose so,' she was forced to admit, reluctantly, not daring to meet his eyes. She was beginning to feel tired and drained and, besides, it was getting later and later. 'I must go,' she said wearily. 'It's no use fighting with each other like this. At least let's part on amicable terms.' She turned and began walking towards the door.

'Where are you going? I'm not finished with you as yet.'

Claire didn't bother to turn around; she couldn't face being skewered by his eyes any longer. She just wanted to get out, get away. She carried on walking, feeling rather than hearing him as he walked up behind her.

'It's late—you can't cycle back at this hour.'

'Go away. I can cycle back at any damn hour I please.'

'And look at me when I'm talking to you!' he roared, making her jump, but she refused to give him the satisfaction of looking around. She had been doing what he wanted for way too long as it was. Against all common sense she had been stupid enough to have fallen in love with him, and he had manipulated her love to enslave her. When he crooked his finger, she leapt into bed with him. He called the shots and she danced to his tune.

She pulled open the front door, no mean feat considering its weight, and he slammed it back shut before she could walk out, his face thunderously angry. This time she did turn around and look at him, her back against the massive door.

'Stop bossing me about!' she said, exploiting her new-found courage to the limit. She had never seen him as livid as he was now, but then again, she had never stood up to him with such hostile vehemence. In time, she thought, I'll laugh about this. Right now, though, she was quaking inside, even though her chin was stubborn and her eyes stormy.

He towered over her, his brows drawn together, his mouth tight with anger.

'What the hell has got into you?' he thundered. 'You've never been like this before! I thought you were sweet and innocent and uncomplicated.'

'Well, you can't be right all the time,' Claire responded quickly, 'and if you keep up the shouting you'll have the housekeeper down to see what the hell's going on.'

That only made him angrier. 'I don't care if the whole damn county comes to investigate!' he informed her, making no effort to control his voice.

'Well, I do.' She turned to open the door, half expecting him to slam it shut again, but he didn't and she stepped outside, bracing herself as the cold wrapped around her in an icy sheet.

Her bicycle was leaning against the wall and she reached for it, but, before she could hop on, it was snatched from her and was being carried off, towards the side of the manor.

Claire stared at him, open-mouthed, then she ran after him furiously.

'Give me back my bike!' she wailed. She felt like stamping her feet in frustration or else screaming at the top of her voice, but she did neither. 'Where are you going?' she demanded, running behind him, and he said grimly, 'To my car. You're damn well not cycling back at this time of the night.'

His car. Where was it? Parked, she saw soon enough, at the side of the house, and almost entirely obscured by the trees and shrubbery. Normally it was parked out front, in the courtyard, which was why she had initially assumed that he wasn't in when she had rung the doorbell.

He opened it with a button on his key-ring and yanked open the boot, shoving her bike inside then slamming shut the boot. Claire stood staring at the closed boot in helpless frustration.

'Get in,' he said, opening the passenger door and then walking around to slip into the driver's seat.

Over my dead body, she wanted to retort, but then that was all well and good, but he had the upper hand, didn't he? In the absence of her bike she could hardly walk back, it would take forever, and there was no way that she was going to demean herself by asking for the cottage keys after she had stormed into the house and practically slammed them down his throat. Oh, no, that would certainly give him the last laugh, wouldn't it?

She remained standing, biting her lip with indecision, until it felt as though hypothermia was beginning to set in. With bad grace she deposited herself in the seat and the door was hardly shut before the car was pulling away.

She looked covertly at the hard profile and then looked away, aware that her heart was being very erratic.

'I'm staying at Karen's house,' she said into the silence, and briefly gave him directions on how to get there, to which she received no acknowledgement, and she pursed her lips and stared out of the window, watching the dark outlines of trees and fields and houses swishing past.

The car turned sharply into the left-hand lane and she stiffened in alarm.

'This isn't the way,' she said, and his mouth curled into a smile.

'I told you, I'm not finished with you as yet.'

He pulled into a small path that wound away from the side road into open fields and killed the engine, turning to face her with one arm extended along the back of the seat. She found that she was perspiring slightly, nervous and apprehensive even though she knew that she had nothing to fear from him, not physically at any rate.

'I grew up with her,' he said at last, breaking the silence which had been stretching between them like elastic. 'At least, she had been around for as long as I can remember, a pretty girl who blossomed into a beautiful woman.'

Claire stared at him, wishing that it weren't so dark in the car because she would have liked to have seen the expression on his face. His voice told her nothing, it was carefully controlled, expressionless.

'Olivia?'

'You wanted to know about her, didn't you?' he said mockingly. 'Well, I'll tell you. I never really noticed her until she was nearly twenty, not sexually at any rate.'

Claire winced at that. She could imagine him falling in love with the leggy blonde, his green eyes devouring her in that way he had, telling her that he wanted her, a mixture of deadly charm and blatant invitation that could devastate. He had a way of communicating what he wanted without saying a word, and how could any woman resist that?

'And then what happened?' she asked in a strange voice, feeling like a voyeur, but needing to hear everything, absolutely everything that he was prepared to divulge about her.

'The inevitable. I slept with her. We were married shortly after. In the end, it was something of a whirlwind romance, even though I'd known her in passing for years.'

'The photo was taken on your wedding-day.'

'Yes.' He paused. 'I liked having it there, at hand, to remind me of other times.'

Claire swallowed painfully. Memories of the past and dreams of the future were the stuff that life was built on. He had memories of the past, but the dreams of the future had died the day his wife had. Wasn't that what it amounted to? There was no room at the inn for *her*.

'Is that why you never married,' she asked, 'because of your wife?'

'I suppose you could say that.' He shrugged his broad shoulders.

'How did she ... how was she ...'

'Killed?' Out in the open the word sounded bleak and slightly offensive, like an oath uttered in a church. 'She was driving back home one night, one very rainy night. It was late and dark and she lost control on one of the sharper bends. She was always inclined to use the roads as her own personal race-track.' He gave a mirthless laugh. 'I was told that death would have been instantaneous.'

'I'm so sorry,' Claire murmured.

'And satisfied, I hope? Now that I've explained about it all, maybe we can just let the matter rest?' He started up the engine, reversing out of the path. In his mind, she knew, it was now resolved. She knew about Olivia, she knew fully his reasons for not wanting involvement, so no more problem. She would accept his terms once again and they would be back to square one.

He began driving back to the manor and she said sharply, 'Wrong direction. I told you, I'm going to Karen's house. I shall be staying there until I can find somewhere permanent of my own.'

She felt infinitely safer saying that with him behind the steering-wheel. He looked at her with a harsh frown, as though he couldn't quite believe his ears.

'Stop being a fool!'

'I have,' she retorted. 'I did the minute I decided to end our relationship.'

He didn't slow down. She glanced at him furtively from under her lashes, wondering whether she would be subjected to another blistering torrent of wrath, but nothing. His face remained averted and she began to feel wary at the lack of reaction. Of course, she told herself, this is much better, it means that what I'm saying has finally sunk in, and he's accepting it.

'I'll collect the stuff from the cottage tomorrow. I had planned on calling Karen across to give me a hand this evening, but I didn't manage to finish on time, and I thought that since I wasn't going to be staying there the night, I'd lock up the cottage and return the key to you. I should have kept it, I suppose. It would have been more logical, wouldn't it? As it is, I'll have to fetch it off Mrs Evans tomorrow evening after work. Silly me.' She was rambling on and her voice abruptly petered out.

'I was right about you, wasn't I?' he rasped, ignoring her long-winded monologue, and she looked at him, surprised.

'What do you mean?'

'You want marriage—you've always wanted marriage.'

'And what's wrong with that?' Claire burst out defensively, not bothering to disguise it. 'Yes, I want marriage, kids, the works! I thought that I could live with you, no questions asked, but I couldn't, especially not now that I've found out about Olivia.'

'No,' he said in a smooth, cold voice, 'especially not now.' They were approaching Karen's house and he slowed down until he had pulled to a halt outside, then he faced her, his face icy and disdainful.

'What are you implying?' she asked, bewildered.

'I always wondered what a talented girl like you was doing working as a cleaner, but you were so convincing, weren't you, with all that rubbish about loving beautiful things and loving to be surrounded by them. I looked at that fresh, innocent, blushing face of yours and I actually, for the first time, asked myself whether I wasn't being over-suspicious. After all, suspicion is one of those pieces of baggage that every wealthy man is forced to carry on his shoulders; it becomes a habit that guides everything you do, every response you make. But you were clever, weren't you? Not overtly glamorous, no designer clothes, the right little noises of refusal every time any present was offered to you.'

Claire felt her body turning to stone. She knew what he was saying but she couldn't say a thing, her mouth simply wouldn't function.

'You threw yourself at me and I thought, no, no scheming woman would be that obvious. If you were a gold-digger, you would have played hard to get, hoped that your girlish naïveté would arouse my interest.'

'You're wrong,' she denied, horrified. 'I don't know how you can think those things.'

'You knew that I wasn't looking for marriage, but you hoped you would be able to convince me that I was wrong, didn't you? But then you found that picture and now that you know the whole story, now that you see that I really am deadly serious about steering clear of involvement with any woman, you've decided to cut your losses and run.'

She swung round and began groping for the door-handle and he yanked her back to face him.

'Truth hurts, doesn't it, Claire?' he sneered. 'You played your game and you lost.'

She looked at that hard, sensuous face, his eyes glittering in the darkness of the car, and she couldn't find a thing to say.

'Until you found that picture, you were warm and yielding. Overnight you changed. What a breathtaking coincidence.'

'You don't understand!' But he ignored that. She wondered whether he had heard her protest at all.

'Did you get a kick out of making a fool of me? No woman has done that before! Did the thought of that turn you on?' His fingers were biting into her and she had to stop herself from crying out in pain. 'Let's just see how indifferent you are, shall we? Let me just see how much was real and how much was pretence.'

He pulled her towards him and his mouth met hers with a force that sent her head reeling back. With one hand he cupped the back of her neck; the other held her head so that her efforts to escape were fruitless. She closed her eyes and groaned as his lips forced hers to part.

He whispered something against her mouth, but she didn't catch what he said. I don't want to respond to this, she told herself desperately, but her senses were fighting a losing battle with her brain, and the heat that his touch had stirred in her overwhelmed her until her hands wound round his neck and she frantically kissed him back, no longer caring about the stupidity of what she was doing. He knew her body so well, he knew what she liked, and he used the knowledge ruthlessly, finding her breast and caressing it roughly until she wanted to cry out.

It was a dark street, and at this hour of the night there wasn't a soul around. Theirs was one car sandwiched between many, invisible, not that James seemed to notice one way or the other.

He hoisted her jumper up and undid the buttons of her blouse and she caressed his dark head as he bent to lick her hardened nipples, sending shivers of excitement through her.

She no longer gave a damn what happened tomorrow, she just wanted that passionate unison of their bodies.

When he pulled down her jumper and drew back, she looked at him, dazed.

'Point proved,' he said softly. 'It's gratifying to know that at least in that area you weren't pretending.'

'You bastard,' she said. He was sitting back against the door, his face shadowed, his lips curled in satisfaction and she had to stop herself from striking out at him. 'Yes,' she said, buttoning her blouse with shaky fingers, 'you proved your point. Now will you sleep better tonight?'

She threw open the car door and snatched her bag from the ground and, as she let herself into the house with the key that Karen had lent her, she didn't look back.

CHAPTER FIVE

Two days later, she received a call from Jackie. At the office, despite the fact that she had spent months telling her sister that personal calls were frowned upon. It was all water off a duck's back, of course. If Jackie wanted to get in touch, and it just so happened that the inclination fell some time between the hours of eight-thirty and five-thirty, then ring the office she would, without a moment's hesitation.

'How are you?'

Claire heard her sister's authoritarian voice down the end of the line with a certain amount of foreboding. Experience had taught her to decipher the various undertones her sister unconsciously used, and right now there was something vaguely meaningful about the greeting, so she frowned and said without preamble, 'I can't talk, Jack, Tony's lurking around, ready to pounce.'

'I'll have to meet this Tony,' Jackie replied smoothly. 'He seems to spend all his time, according to you, lurking around, ready to pounce. Doesn't the man do any work?'

'He thinks on his feet,' Claire murmured vaguely, liking her sister's tone of voice less and less.

'And in front of your desk, from the sounds of it. Are you sure he's not giving you the eye? You know how incredibly naïve you can be sometimes.'

'Don't be ridiculous!' Claire defended, grinning reluctantly at that inaccurate shot in the dark. 'Tony's more attracted to himself than he is to me.'

There was a pause and Claire waited patiently for the inevitable enquiry into her frame of mind. Jackie was solicitous to the point of smothering sometimes. She didn't want sympathy, though, not even of the well meaning variety. All she wanted was to forget that James Forrester had ever existed. If she could have somehow contracted a temporary bout of amnesia, she would have grabbed at it because thoughts of him were driving her mad, even though she knew that the best thing she had ever done, for her own state of mental well-being, was to have walked out on their abortive relationship. It was funny how she could hurt and yet still remain strong enough to realise that she was simply hurting from the inevitable.

'How are you, Claire?' her sister asked. 'Really?'

'Fine.'

'You don't sound fine.'

'Jackie,' she began, getting a little impatient, 'I honestly can't afford to spend too much time on the phone, chatting. I've got heaps of work to get through.'

'What you mean is that you don't want to talk about *him*. I understand. Enough said. I'd probably have been exactly the same. Not,' she couldn't resist adding, to Claire's amusement, 'that I would ever have allowed myself to become involved with a man who hadn't got me way up at the very top of his list of priorities. Tom would never have used me as a bed companion. He wouldn't have *dared*.'

Tom was her husband, a thoroughly nice man, and Claire wondered how he would react if he knew that his wife was quietly making him out to be henpecked. He wasn't henpecked at all, as far as Claire had ever seen. He just knew how to handle Jackie. He gave her free rein to do as she pleased, just as long as it suited him.

In his own good-natured, amiable way he never allowed her to stray too far.

'You can be rather commanding,' Claire murmured, her attention straying to the layout she was working on. It needed a few touches to complete it and she began doodling them in.

'Anyway,' Jackie said in a businesslike voice, 'I won't keep you any longer. The prowling boss is already probably on his way over to your desk to club you over the head for having spent four and a half minutes on the telephone when you should be doing your drawing...'

Claire smiled at that. Jackie had always thought of her job as doing a spot of drawing, like a child dabbling about with crayons in a kindergarten class. She had no idea how long it took her to perfect her lettering, or to rework her layouts when Tony threw them back at her with some vague request to make the 'whole thing a little more modern', or 'take out some of the colour. We want subtle not sizzling.'

Jackie had an undemanding part-time job at a gallery, and it suited her fine. It gave her the opportunity to earn a little bit of money, though she hardly needed to given Tom's income, and it also fitted in with Freddie, her four-year-old son, who was endearingly hyperactive and could reduce her to a dithering wreck faster than anyone else.

'I just wanted to make sure that you were all right. Not thinking of doing anything silly.'

'Yes, I'm fine,' Claire said, doodling furiously on her layout.

'Good. Oh, just one last thing. We're having a little party this Saturday, and I think it might be a good idea if you came along.'

'No, Jackie, honestly, you know...'

'No more than twenty people, and quite a few eligible young men. There's no point pining away up there in the back of beyond.'

'I'm not pining! And Reading isn't the back of beyond. In fact, I have some very good friends around here. I'll make sure that I go...'

'Kicks off around eight-thirty. I'll meet you at the station, as per usual. When are you ever going to get a car? Why don't you come down in the morning and we can do a spot of shopping. Buy some nice clothes instead of your usual uniform of jeans and jumpers.'

'No, I...'

'OK. I'll see you in the evening, then. Catch the six-thirty train, then you can give me a hand with everything. And please wear something dressy?'

Claire opened her mouth to protest and heard the dead sound of the dialling tone.

So that, she thought, had been the object of the phone call. Jackie wanted to rescue her from a life of maudlin moping about, and, in her usual organisational way, fix her up with some thoroughly suitable young man. That didn't provide too much of a headache because she had no intention of going to any party, nor had she any intention of being fixed up with one of her sister's protégés. A bit nearer the day, towards the end of the week, she would phone and make her excuses. Flu was always a reasonable alibi in cases like this.

She promptly forgot about the invitation and spent the remainder of the day trying hard to concentrate on what she was doing.

They were having a busy period. Tony was rushing about the office like a mad chicken, tearing his hair out with a theatricality which suggested that at least part of it was put on. She barely had time to look up from her drawing-board, which was something of a relief since it took her mind off things to some extent.

They had been volunteered, without exception, to work overtime and by the time Claire stood up, stretched her legs and began packing away her paper and pencils, it was after eight and already dark outside.

Tony shot her a look which suggested that eight o'clock was hardly an acceptable time for departure, considering everyone else would be working for at least another hour, and Claire met his stare with a polite but firm smile.

Just you dare saunter over here, she thought, and say anything. Little Miss Obliging Claire Harper was no more, a fact which he would rediscover soon enough if he even so much as suggested that she was deserting her post.

He must have read the expression on her face, though, because he made no attempt to stop her and she left the office with a little feeling of triumph.

It was another cold night and she pulled her jacket around her as she stepped outside. At this hour, Reading town centre was not a particularly pleasant place to be. The offices were largely deserted and a different crowd emerged to fill the streets. Young boys with weird haircuts and girls in tight skirts and high heels. All perfectly harmless, no doubt, but they made Claire feel edgy. She jumped on to her bike and was about to cycle off to Karen's house when she heard the sharp beeping of a horn.

Of course she had no intention of looking around. She headed off and within minutes was aware of being followed by a car, cruising along with its headlights beaming down on her.

Now she was more angry than scared. She stopped, jumped off her bike and spun around to be confronted by James, who had stepped out of the car and was standing on the pavement watching her. There was a light, cold breeze blowing and it gave him a tousled, rakish look, despite the fact that he was still wearing his suit.

'What,' she spluttered furiously, 'the hell do you think you're doing?'

Had it only been a matter of hours since she had last seen him? she wondered. He seemed taller than ever, more powerful. She couldn't make out the expression on his face, it was too dark for that, but she could see the hard-boned, aggressive lines and it sent a little forbidden shiver through her. It was a reaction which she stifled almost as soon as it had appeared. Once she would have let that little shiver control her, send her foolish heart spinning, but that seemed like a long time ago. Now she was developing that hard edge born out of bitterness and necessity which would give her protection against treacherous emotions.

Every nerve in her body seemed to have moved into another gear, though, and she still had to force herself to appear cool and polite.

She had no intention of forgetting his little amusing game yesterday at her expense. Turn the key and watch her react, then stand back and snigger, all to prove a point.

'Didn't you hear me blow my horn?' he asked, leaning casually on the open door and surveying her.

'I heard *somebody* blowing their horn,' Claire answered. 'I assumed that if it had been someone I knew, they would have identified themselves. Though why should you? I suppose you assume that you're exempt from little acts of courtesy like that.' She hopped back on her bike and threw over her shoulder in the same freezing voice, 'I'm surprised you didn't just blow a whistle and expect me to come running and salute.'

He didn't answer. She heard his car door slam, then the squeal of tyres as he accelerated in front of her, blocking her path, forcing her to dismount.

Claire looked at him furiously and began hoisting her bike on to the pavement, but he pushed open his door and ushered her forcefully to the passenger seat.

'Take your hands off me!' she yelled, attracting a few stares which didn't seem to bother him in the slightest, even though they bothered her quite a bit. She found herself lowering her voice and glaring at him accusingly.

'You can't just swan along here and…and accost me!'

'I'll put that thing you call a bike in the boot.' He opened the passenger door and pushed her in, then slammed the door behind her.

Claire sat there, fuming, waiting, then, as soon as he had sat down next to her in the driver's seat, she turned to him, spitting fury.

'Very macho,' she snapped, twisting to look at him. The engine was still running, that distinctive deep-throated purr made by very powerful cars, but he wasn't about to move off. His hands weren't even on the steering-wheel. They were clasped behind his head as he leaned against the door and looked at her in a way that seemed to say, All right, if you want to yell, go ahead and get it out of your system. That made her even more speechless with anger.

'I could report you for kidnapping,' she said wildly because he was unnerving her with that shuttered stare of his.

'Don't be ridiculous.'

'Well, I'm certainly not sitting here of my own free will! What are you doing here, anyway?'

'I always wondered what your office looked like.'

She had no idea what that remark was supposed to mean and she gave him a look that said, Oh, really, you must think I was born yesterday. 'That's news to me,' she said coolly. 'You never expressed the slightest bit of interest in where I worked before. Maybe that would have been a little too familiar for your liking? After all, we were only sleeping together. Why on earth should you give a damn about my life outside the bed?'

'You're exaggerating,' he drawled with an unsmiling face. 'Of course I knew what you did for a living.'

'Oh, yes,' Claire said sarcastically, 'I forgot. You did. After all, I spent long enough enthusiastically telling you all about my job. What fun you must have found that. You still haven't told me what you're doing here.'

'When do you intend to collect the rest of your things from the cottage?'

That hurt. He wanted her out, but did he have to be so damned blunt about it?

'As soon as possible,' she said stiffly. 'I would have collected it after work this afternoon, but Tony asked me to work overtime.'

'Oh, Tony asked you to do that, did he?' James said in a voice that made her flush. 'And what else does Tony ask you to do, out of interest?'

'You have a disgusting mind.'

'Is that how you'd describe it? I would say worldly-wise.' He was watching her intently. He looked away, staring out of the window for a while, then, without speaking, he slipped the car into gear and pulled away from the kerb.

He knew the way back to Karen's house without having to be reminded of the directions and Claire sat in an uncomfortable silence, hating being this close to him, but nevertheless feeding off his presence, off that electricity that seemed to radiate out of him. It wasn't fair. She was beginning to get to grips with her situation, wasn't she? Why did he have to come along and sabotage all her groundwork?

'You used to work a fair amount of overtime when we were seeing each other,' James said lazily, flicking her a sideways glance. 'All at Tony's request?'

'No,' Claire snapped, as the car pulled up to the kerb and he switched off the engine to face her. 'Sometimes I volunteered the overtime myself.'

His face didn't change, but the expression in his eyes hardened. 'They say that bosses can have an awful lot of sex appeal, because of their position.' He tapped the keys dangling in the ignition, lightly. 'A bit like the way a doctor invariably has a supply of adoring patients somewhere in the background. I never paid too much attention to what you used to tell me about Tony, but I can remember his name cropping up frequently enough.'

'I work for him. Of course, his name was going to crop up.'

The green eyes, fringed with black lashes, shot her a brooding look. 'Of course. Now, though, I wonder whether I should have been a bit more suspicious.'

'You're right,' Claire said on a sigh, 'you should have been more suspicious. We've been indulging in a torrid affair for months. In fact, we can't keep our hands off each other!'

Something dangerous flickered in his eyes, but then he glanced down and it was obvious that he was amused by her response.

'When do you want me out of the cottage?' she asked. 'I'm tired and I don't feel inclined to spend the remainder of the night sitting in this car squabbling with you.'

'You've really changed, haven't you, Claire?' he asked in an odd voice.

'You make that sound like an insult,' she said, looking away. She hated this drag of her senses that she felt whenever she was near him, this compelling urge to be near him even though they really had nothing further to say to one another. She realised that she was clenching and unclenching her fists and she had to make an effort to sit still and calm. It was all so much easier being reasonable and logical and pleased with herself when he wasn't around.

'You've shed some of that wide-eyed trust.'

Claire shrugged. 'Don't we all, at some point?' She met his eyes steadily. 'Maybe I picked that up from you, a little trait of yours that rubbed off. Not that I can picture you ever being the trusting sort. Were you? Did your wife's death turn you into the person you are today or were you always suspicious and cynical?'

His mouth tightened and she could see in the shadows that his face was clenched in anger.

Where was this light-headed courage coming from? she wondered. He was right. She had changed and she couldn't believe that she had ever been that naïve, innocent girl. She had thrown herself at him, been so eager to please; was it any great surprise that he had accepted what she had bent over backwards to hand him on a silver plate?

'Experiences made me the man I am now,' he said. He reached out and, before she could stop him, his hand was on her chin, forcing her to look at him. 'Not that you ever seemed too dissatisfied with me—or should I say with what I could do for you?' His eyes flicked to her mouth and she read the sensual demand there with detachment. Was he trying to prove, yet again, that he still had a great deal of power over her, despite what she said?

'When,' she said calmly, even though her heart was hammering, 'did you say you wanted me out?'

'I didn't and I don't. A business acquaintance from America is going to be here for a few weeks, but I can always make alternative arrangements if you want to stay on. We're both adults, and let's not beat about the bush here: I want you and the feeling's mutual. So why throw what we have to the winds because of some misguided sense of morality?' His voice was husky, full of that smouldering charm that could knock you sideways.

She just hoped that he wasn't going to try and kiss her. It was bad enough keeping up this mimicry of self-control, but she knew that if those firm, warm lips descended on hers there was a good chance of her precious self-control being blown to bits.

'You mean you'd sleep with me even though you think I was after your money?' She injected incredulity into her voice.

'Yes,' he replied bluntly. 'I would.'

'How flattering for me!' she exclaimed with an icy smile. His face was inches away from hers, and she had to steel herself against the disturbing images that threatened to grab her by the throat. Images of them in bed together, talking, laughing, eating out in various pubs and restaurants. Had he enjoyed any of those things or were they necessary evils to be borne in his game of seduction? If he had kept his wife a secret from her, then what else had he been hiding?

'I wouldn't dream of putting you through that crisis of conscience, though,' she added soothingly. 'So you'd better start looking for someone else to share your bed. I'll collect my things tomorrow, and now——' she drew back and flipped open the car door '—if you'll excuse me? And,' she said, turning to face him, 'another thing. Please don't come near me again.'

'Why?' he taunted softly. 'Afraid that you might give in?' His hand shot out and he pulled her forward by her hair. 'Don't think you're going to get away from me, Claire. What we have between us isn't yet finished.'

'That's a matter of opinion.'

'No. It's a matter of fact.'

His green eyes threatened and she backed out of the car hurriedly, preferring to ignore that rather than argue the point. She had hardly climbed out when he pulled away with a screech of tyres and was gone so quickly that she had to convince herself that he had ever been there.

She let herself into the house quietly. There were no lights on and she thought that perhaps Karen had decided to indulge in an early night, but her bedroom door was wide open, and she realised that her flatmate had gone out.

She ran a bath and stretched out in it, her eyes closed, furiously thinking back to that little scene that had taken place between James and herself earlier.

There had been no need for him to accost her at her place of employment. He could always have picked up the telephone and called her about removing her things. That way, he wouldn't have had to lay eyes on her. But, she now realised, that wouldn't have suited him at all. Unfinished business, he had called their relationship, and that about summed it up. He might not intend making a commitment to her, but that didn't mean that he didn't want her in his life. He just didn't want her demanding anything. And when it came to ending their affair he wanted to be the one to do it.

She stepped out of the bath and wrapped her hair in a turban, still preoccupied with her thoughts. They went round and round in her head until she began to feel quite dizzy.

Did he think that he could continue turning up, disrupting her life, whenever he felt like it? There was no way that she would end up a nervous wreck because of him. She had spent too long with downbent head, passively accepting his terms and conditions. He knew how attracted she had been to him and still was, despite all his theorising about her being a gold-digger, and he must think that she would be a pushover.

And when he was ready to discard her he would do so without a backward glance, because his emotions had never been involved.

Well, she wasn't about to give him that chance. If he turned up at the house, she would tell Karen to inform him that she wasn't home, and if he dared to turn up at the office, well she would be OK there. With people around, there was a limit to the amount of damage he could inflict.

The following day she left work on time, despite Tony's heavy frown, and arrived at the cottage in good time. She had booked a taxi to come for her and her meagre possessions at precisely six-thirty, which would give her ample time to make sure that nothing was being left behind.

It was a jolt returning there, even though she had only been out of the place for a matter of days.

She had to make herself check each room efficiently, in a businesslike manner, and not mope around, thinking about those halcyon days when her love for him had seemed strong enough to carry her through anything.

She was halfway through when she heard the key being inserted in the door, and she froze.

There was only one person it could possibly be. Of all the bad luck and even worse timing in the world! She flew down the stairs, already primed for attack, to be confronted by a woman whom she had never seen in her life before. Tall, well proportioned, with a mass of blonde hair gathered at the back into a neatly arranged chignon. Some silky strands had escaped and wisped around her face, giving the only hint that this woman was sexier than she wanted to portray herself, at least in the working environment.

Claire didn't know who was the more surprised, her or the blonde. They stared at each other for a matter of a few seconds, then the woman recovered her composure and said in a clipped American accent that she had come to see the cottage.

'James sent me,' she said, looking around her. 'I've come straight from London.' She began browsing through the small sitting-room, eyeing everything meticulously like a prospective house buyer instead of a tenant. 'I absolutely flew up so that I could make it here while it was still light. By the way, my name's Gayle King. You must be...' She looked at Claire for the first time, her lips parted in a polite smile even though her eyes were warm and assessing, not unfriendly. 'What's the name? Ah yes, Harper, isn't it? Something Harper, aren't I right? James said you might be here collecting your stuff.' She shifted her glance to the assortment of bags and boxes stacked by the front door. 'You travel

light, don't you?' she said, as though that was some sort
of eccentricity. 'I positively crate things around with
me—clothes, shoes, you name it. I came over from
America with one trunkload of suits alone!' She began
moving upstairs and Claire found herself following.

She had always wondered what James's type of woman
was. All men had a type, and she knew that she hadn't
been his, because he had informed her on countless oc-
casions, sometimes with amusement, sometimes with a
wry grin, that she was nothing like the women he had
been out with in the past. Was Gayle King his type? All
blonde hair and long legs and easy conversation?

'How long do you intend to be over here?' Claire
asked, and Gayle replied, without turning around, continuing to look over the small bedroom with its flowery
quilted bedspread and sunny wallpaper.

'A few weeks, hence the temporary accommodation.
I wouldn't normally have moved this far out of London
but most of my jobs involve companies in the Thames
Valley, and of course——' she looked at Claire with a
wry smile '—James can be very persuasive, which is why
I'm here at all. I don't normally go for cottages. I prefer
a cleaner, more high-tech look.'

'High-tech, yes,' Claire said faintly. 'How long have
you known him?'

'Years. We met, actually, when I worked for a firm
of stockbrokers in New York. Then he wooed me over
to his company, to take over as the financial consultant
for one of his subsidiaries in Chicago——' she gave a
warm laugh which sent a shudder through Claire '—and
I haven't looked back since! I hope I'm not shoving you
out of this place?'

Claire shook her head. Years? He had known her for *years*? She had to turn away because she was sure that despair would be written all over her face.

'I was...I've already moved out, actually.' She cleared her throat and tried to look cheery. 'I only came to collect my belongings.'

Gayle looked relieved. 'Good,' she said. 'Incentive or not, I wouldn't have moved in here if it entailed your moving out. Not, of course, that James would allow that. He's got a heart of gold.'

That was news to her, and she tried not to look stunned.

'Has he? I wouldn't know.'

'Oh, yes.' The inspection of the upper floor was over and Gayle carefully went downstairs, watching her feet carefully because she was wearing very high heels and the stairs were hopelessly ungenerous. 'Not that he likes it much in evidence.'

'No,' Claire said, more depressed by the minute. 'You must know him very well.'

'We've made an effort to keep in touch,' she replied airily. 'We worked very closely together for a while, when I worked at Carter and Co., and it just sort of grew from there.'

'Carter and Co.? My brother-in-law works for them, if it's the same company! What a coincidence.'

'What's his name?'

'Tom. Thomas Barnet.' But Gayle crinkled her forehead and shook her head. He must have joined the company after she had left, she said, and the conversation was dropped. With relief, Claire didn't pick up the pieces. She had had enough of chatting about James, anyway. She didn't want to continue hearing about this marvellous friendship that had apparently transcended all barriers of culture and distance, and besides, the taxi was due any minute. She peered out of the window and right on cue, it pulled up outside the cottage.

Claire turned to say goodbye and Gayle gave her a rueful look.

'Perhaps you could drop by for coffee some time,' she said and Claire nodded politely. Drop by for coffee? Be regaled with some more stories about James? Who knew, by then Gayle might well be sleeping with him, and would be full of tales of how their marvellous, wonderful, uplifting damned friendship had mellowed into a marvellous, wonderful, uplifting physical relationship. No, thanks, Claire wanted to say, I'd prefer to have coffee with a local resident at Reading Gaol. Which, she had to admit, was a bit of a shame, because Gayle didn't seem too bad. On the whole. Was it her fault that she was brainy, beautiful, extrovert and had known James for years?

It was just something else to contend with on top of her general despondency, though.

She had settled down well enough in Karen's house, but it was nothing like the cottage. She kept drawing comparisons all the time. Everything was different, none of it for the better. She realised that she had become attached to the warm faded glow of the beams in the cottage, the old, soft furnishings, the outdated utensils in the kitchen.

And more, a little voice whispered in her ear. Wasn't James the real reason that nothing seemed right? His absence was like a hole inside her, a constant reminder that she was drifting aimlessly now that he was no longer around. It was a shock to realise just how much her life had been focused on him. She would find herself staring into space, remembering every single little detail about him, the way he smiled, the way he frowned, the way he used to rake his fingers impatiently through his hair whenever he was irritated. The images tripped her up just when she least expected it, pulled the rug from under her feet, and then she had to rebuild all that hard-won confidence in herself.

She made sure to put on a bright face, though, whenever someone was looking at her. She especially didn't want Karen to become too concerned about her, because Karen, by nature, was a caring person, and Claire had a feeling that at the slightest hint of depression she would be taken under her wing and tended to like an ailing bird.

The only time she felt free to be herself was in bed at night, and ever since that meeting with Gayle at the cottage she had found herself lying in her room, in darkness, wondering what they were getting up to. Were they sleeping together? Had she slept with him in the past? Maybe she was an old flame as well as an old friend. It could be that theirs was one of those convenient arrangements whereby they slept together occasionally, when it suited them, but felt free to do their own thing in each other's absence. A sort of open relationship. Maybe, Claire thought, depressed, I was just filling a gap until they could renew their love-affair. Who knows? He had never mentioned Gayle to her, not even in passing, but that didn't say much considering he had also never mentioned his wife.

The rush of work which had kept her busy at the office and which had initially helped to take her mind off James had abated, and she now found herself at a loose end in the evenings, not tired enough to go to bed but too lethargic to do anything much.

On the Friday evening, on the spur of the moment, she called her sister and said, without preamble, 'I've decided to come to your party tomorrow after all. I knew you'd be surprised,' she continued, when there was silence at the other end, and she heard Jackie laugh sheepishly.

'Well, you know I've always had to force you into one of these things in the past. Why the sudden change of heart?'

'Why not?' Claire hedged lightly, hearing her sister's brain begin whirring away as it digested her reply and her tone of voice.

'So the healing process hasn't begun, then,' she said drily, and Claire sighed, grimacing.

'Of course it has. But slowly.'

'I see. Well, a good party will take your mind off things. There'll be a good supply of eligible males around.' She carried on before Claire could protest at that, 'Buy yourself something new. I always find that a spending spree is a very good way of curing depression.'

'You've never been depressed in your life, Jackie, and anyway I can't afford a spending spree. Don't forget you've got Tom indulgently paying your bills.'

'So I have,' Jackie agreed smugly, 'in which case, you could always make it a cheap spending spree.'

Claire had to grin at that one and she rang off a moment later, after they had arranged a meeting point.

The following morning, she decided to follow her sister's advice and do some shopping. She had had another restless night. At one mad point, she could remember with a sense of shame actually considering cycling over to Frilton Manor and lurking around just to glimpse James in passing. In the dark, silent bedroom, she had dwelt on this fantasy in such detail that it had seemed quite real in the end. He would be looking the same as ever, tall, lean, vital, but just when she got to the point in the fantasy when he would, on closer inspection, appear a little drawn, obviously pining, she remembered Gayle King's presence and the fantasy deviated into an agonising picture of the two of them, laughing, exchanging intimate little jokes, making love.

She threw herself into shopping the following morning with gusto. It was time to start forgetting James Forrester, to start rebuilding her life, and an attractive outfit was as good a place to start as any. Jackie had mentioned that there would be some eligible men at her party. Well, Claire thought, she wasn't going to throw herself into bed with any of them—oh, no, *that* would never happen again—but some harmless flirting wouldn't hurt, and it might just remind her stubborn brain that there was life beyond James Forrester.

It was easy shopping in Reading. There weren't that many shops that she found appealing, so her choices were limited. Consequently, there was no dithering. She found what she was looking for virtually in the first shop she went into, and with uncustomary extravagance she paid for the dress without any crises of conscience. It was short, in burnished gold, with a scooped neckline that gave her an air of elegance which her normal garb of jeans certainly did not.

She was going to arrive early at her sister's, and dress there. She cycled back to Karen's house with her bags tucked over the handlebars of her bike, and she couldn't help smiling as she imagined Jackie's reaction to her outfit. Not horror, exactly, more stupefaction.

She was right. She arrived at her sister's house, a fair-sized detached place in North London, with a pleasant, mature garden which was firmly kept in place. Not a weed in sight. Even the tree in the corner was upright, obeying orders, no slouching.

Jackie, not one to let something like a party throw her out of joint, was in control. She had hired a team of caterers to do the food, a finger buffet, which was now spread over the sideboard, each dish covered in clingfilm. There was a bar at the opposite end of the room, with glasses set out on a makeshift table, and Claire knew from experience that apart from the usual shorts there would be a huge supply of exceedingly good wine. Tom loved his wines. He belonged to a wine club, and each crate of wine was carefully chosen and lovingly vetted.

In fact, he seemed a lot more bothered by the whole thing than Jackie. He gave her a brief peck on the cheek, in between knotting his tie and checking the drinks, then murmured something about her looking a trifle casual.

'Don't worry, Tom,' Claire said affectionately, 'I've brought my change of clothes.' She waved her holdall at him and he nodded distractedly, moving off as she was appropriated by her sister and led to the guest room which she normally occupied.

'He's in a dither,' Jackie said, glancing into the mirror on the dressing table and automatically smoothing down her hair. She looked fabulous, in a white silk trouser suit which didn't look cheap and a pair of flat-heeled sandals. Cool, expensive, classy. Claire hoped her little number wasn't going to appear too tawdry. God, the embarrassment. 'There are going to be a lot of clients,' she continued, 'and some representatives from abroad. America, a couple from France. God knows why this couldn't have been held at one of the London hotels, but no, Tom thought that it would be a nice touch to have me slaving over a hot stove.'

'I thought the caterers had done the slaving,' Claire pointed out mildly, and Jackie grinned.

'You know what I mean. I'll leave you to get dressed.' She eyed the holdall cryptically. 'And I hope you do me proud.'

Oh, yes, Claire thought as she stood in front of the full-length mirror forty minutes later, you won't recognise me. Shame, she thought, that James wasn't around. He might have realised that it wasn't just her personality that had changed, it was everything.

CHAPTER SIX

CLAIRE hadn't noticed his arrival at all.

She had emerged from her bedroom, having spent ages painstakingly applying her make-up and scrutinising herself in the mirror. She wanted to make sure that everything was all right because she felt awkward in the dress. It really wasn't her sort of attire at all. It was very dramatic, but she decided that too much was exposed; it was just too clingy—not that there was much that she could do about that. And anyway, it was obviously the right choice for this sort of do, because Jackie had circled her four times in the bedroom, clearly impressed.

She had walked into the lounge, which was already humming nicely with twenty or so people, with more arriving by the minute, despite Jackie's original assurances that it was going to be a small affair, and she had immediately caused a sensation. A couple of the women there she knew from old, and they were open with their friendly curiosity, and the remainder she could feel staring at her, trying to work out whether they should ignore the possible threat or introduce themselves and check out the situation first-hand. It was a novel sensation, and rather enjoyable, she discovered, after the initial discomfort.

So it was a bit of a surprise when someone whispered into her ear, 'You look ravishing. Where have you been all my life?' and she looked around, startled, to find herself staring into two very blue, very assessing, eyes. A few months ago she would have blushed at this blatant introduction, but ever since she had walked out on James she had slowly found herself cultivating the art of pretence, even when she was a mass of confusion inside, and she called upon her new-found knowledge now, smiling politely, coolly, making sure that he got the message that she was not up for grabs.

And from the look in his eyes she knew that he had got her unspoken message, but that didn't stop him plying her with charm for most of the evening.

His name was Stephen Hancock, Steve to friends, and with an ease which she could only admire he proceeded to regale her with unasked-for details of himself.

He was from New York, he informed her in a voice that implied that New York was, in fact, the only place to be, and he was a stockbroker. He worked for the New York branch of Tom's company, Carter and Co., and he was, he managed to tell her in so many words, only thirty but upwardly very mobile indeed.

She eyed him with amusement, thinking that he certainly seemed to possess all the upwardly very mobile accoutrements, including what looked very much like a designer suit, a pair of shoes with a very expensive and easily recognisable logo, and a suntan which, it transpired in the course of conversation, was the product of one week's snatched holiday in the Bahamas.

'Lucky you,' Claire said, not sure whether to like or dislike this brand of effervescence. 'I can't even afford one week's snatched holiday under a sunlamp at the moment, never mind the tropics.'

He laughed at that, and from across the room Jackie caught her eye and winked. Claire ignored her completely. She knew what her sister was thinking, that this was just the sort of young man to replace James

Forrester, and there was no way that she was going to play that game.

It would have helped her case if Stephen had held back more, but he dogged her steps for most of the night, and, after four glasses of wine, she was light-headed enough not to care. He was likeable enough, wasn't he? And he didn't seem to mind the fact that she wasn't telling him anything about herself at all. He seemed, in fact, to be perfectly happy talking about himself, and that suited her just fine.

By the end of the evening, from that pleasant, fuzzy wine-induced stratosphere she was inhabiting, Claire realised that she knew a great deal about Stephen Hancock. If there was anything mysterious about him, then he had done a good job keeping it to himself, because he had come across as a cocky but straightforward man with none of the dark complications that she had come to accept as part and parcel of James. True, she had occasionally found her attention wandering in the middle of one of his anecdotes, but that could have been the fact that her glass had been constantly topped up by one of the very efficient bar staff. And anyway, so what if he was a little self-centred and a bit on the boring side? After James Forrester, self-centred and boring came as very refreshing characteristics.

Nevertheless, when he told her that he would be in London for a couple of months and could he look her up, she shot him an alarmed look.

'No involvement!' he said, raising his hands placatingly, and something at the back of her mind told her that that didn't add up. He was attractive enough, clearly eligible, as he had told her in no uncertain terms, so why would he be satisfied with a hands-off relationship?

Her mind wasn't working properly, though. It was muddled, and she was finding it tricky to work out the logical conclusion to her thoughts, so she gave him a vague smile, and said,

'Sure. Look me up some time.'

'You think I won't,' he laughed, 'but I will. You're interesting, different. You have the body of a woman and the face of a child. I like it.' Was there something wolfish in his grin or was her imagination working overtime? She nodded and made as polite an escape as possible, and by the following Monday had promptly forgotten all about him.

She was clearing her desk that evening, stacking her papers away neatly on to a massive clip file which she used for her first drafts, when a voice spoke from behind her and she swung around, surprised.

The office was quite empty. Tony was in his office, his door slightly ajar, and behind another partition two girls from Accounts were still working away, but apart from them there was no one around. She had decided to work late, partly because she had to redo some lettering she had been working on that morning, but mostly because work was preferable to inactivity. Inactivity bred too many memories.

'What are you doing here?' she asked, and Stephen laughed at the expression on her face.

'I came to see you,' he informed her. 'I phoned your house and a girl there told me that you weren't back from work, and she told me where I could find you, so here I am. You're hard to get hold of, kid, aren't you? I had to get your phone number from your sister; you must have forgotten to give it to me. They don't call me Sherlock Holmes for nothing! And these are for you.' He handed her a bunch of flowers, and she breathed in their aroma, distracted and a little put out by his appearance and by the flowers.

Out of the corner of her eye she could see Tony peering through at them, not making the slightest attempt to disguise his curiosity, and she gave him a bright wave.

She bent down to pick up her bag from the floor and then straightened up, asking him a lot of questions but mostly wanting to find out what he was doing here, *really* doing here. This all seemed a little overkeen and she wasn't thrilled at the prospect of having to defuse a potentially aggravating situation. Hadn't she told him that she wasn't interested in a relationship?

In the cold light of day, she realised that he really was very attractive. His teeth were absolutely perfect, his hair was impeccably combed and he looked terribly well groomed. So what, she couldn't help asking herself again, was he doing here? Tony was still watching them both from his office, wondering what was going on. She had never been one to bring her social life to work.

'I'm surprised you made the trip here all the way from London, just to see me,' she said conversationally, and his eyes skimmed over her once, resting fractionally on her breasts before meeting hers with easy camaraderie.

'Why not? It's not that far. In the old US of A we cover a lot more miles in the space of a day, babe!'

Babe? She smiled weakly and allowed him to usher her towards the door. He was asking her about eating places—were there any bistros? What kind of food did she fancy? French? Chinese? There were some great bars in New York. What about Greek food? Had she ever tried that?

'I really hadn't...' she began, wondering how she could edge herself out of this one, but the apologetic smile died on her lips as she looked up and had her second shock in the space of fifteen minutes. James was standing there, by the outer door. If she had been expecting him, she might have braced herself, but caught off guard she suddenly felt as though the ground had been jerked away from under her.

He was so damned *vital*. She blinked, half expecting him to vanish, but he didn't. He was still standing there, his bright green eyes raking over Stephen, then flicking back to her, cool and expressionless.

He was leaning slightly against the doorframe, his hands in his pockets, and he was so terrifyingly sexy that her mouth went dry. Next to him, Stephen Hancock was the boy next door, a good-looking shell with no substance, none of that fierce aggressiveness that made James so devastating.

'Who's that?' Stephen asked, in the voice of someone sizing up his opponent and finding the odds stacked against him. That brought her back down to earth with a bump.

'No one important,' she said hastily, dragging him towards the door because Tony would be in his element now and she didn't see why she should have her private life made public. Her face felt stiff and her mouth was dry. 'My ex-landlord.'

'Oh, is that all?' He relaxed and linked her arm through his, a gesture which took her by surprise, but she left her hand there, not liking the proprietorial significance behind it but not wanting to make a fuss.

James's mouth had hardened and he continued to stare at her in a way that made her flush angrily. Why should she feel guilty just because she was in the company of another man?

She also resented the way that he remained standing where he was, waiting for them to approach, having the advantage of being able to watch their progress across the room.

'Hello,' she said, when her feet had finally stopped moving and she was standing in front of him. 'What are you doing here?'

'Aren't you going to introduce us, Claire?' he asked in a chillingly polite voice, and she fumbled over an introduction, angry and flustered.

'I'm over here for a secondment,' Stephen elaborated. 'I'm in stockbroking, by the way.'

'Riveting,' James said with freezing politeness.

'I work for Carter and Co.—you may have heard of them? I seem to recognise you. Have we met in the course of business? Who do you work for?'

'The Forrester Group,' James said abruptly, and Stephen nodded.

'Big fish. What do you do there? Manager?'

'Something like that.' He had hardly looked at Stephen during this interchange. His eyes had been fixed on Claire and she had deliberately refused to meet them.

'Something like that! You British! Masters of understatement! We have dealings with some of you guys. Which branch do you manage?'

'All of them.' He tore his eyes away from Claire and looked at Stephen with a touch of restless impatience.

'All of them?' Stephen grinned, raising his eyebrows in disbelief.

'I own the company.'

There was silence as this snippet of information, offhandedly thrown out by James, was digested by Stephen. His face was red, and for the first time he looked uncomfortable and out of his league. He looked sideways at Claire, who had a sudden urge of protectiveness. Stephen had had no idea what he had been up against when he had been introduced to James, and it made her cross to see how he had been demolished in a few throw-away sentences.

'What are you doing here?' she repeated tersely, not meeting his eyes which, she knew, would only remind her of what she had lost.

'You forgot some of your things at the cottage, in your haste to leave the other evening. I have them at the manor.'

'Fine,' Claire said, 'I'll collect them later. They can't be that important because I haven't even missed them.' She glanced at Stephen, and then said, 'I could get them now, if you like. Stephen, would you mind awfully driving me to——?'

'Tomorrow would suit me better,' James cut in smoothly.

'You don't have to be there to supervise,' she returned heatedly and his mouth curled into a smile.

'No, but I'd rather make sure that I were.' Was she supposed to read mistrust behind that statement? she wondered. It would appeal to his sense of humour to know that whether she did or not was immaterial, since she was impotent to launch into a speech of self-defence in front of witnesses.

Tony had now approached them and was surveying the trio with interest. Reluctantly, Claire made the round of introductions, and as soon as James's name was mentioned Tony's face lit up into a broad smile. She knew what was coming. There was something of the born salesman in him and, sure enough, he launched into his rehearsed exposé of what his advertising firm could do for some of James's companies. Put them on the map, make them a household name. He carried this little speech around with him, the way some people carried snapshots of their children, ready to pull it out should the opportunity arise.

Claire groaned inwardly, not knowing where to look, and she was surprised when, at the end of five minutes of self-publicity, James actually appeared to be giving Tony's suggestions some thought.

'I'll be in touch,' he said, and Tony beamed and looked at her with self-satisfaction.

Claire smiled weakly back at him, confused at this turn of events. What did James mean by 'I'll be in touch'? Had it been a throwaway remark or did he really have plans to use their advertising firm?

Tony had strolled off, not wanting to overkill, and Claire edged away from James, automatically pulling Stephen towards the door. James's hooded eyes followed the movement, but he didn't say anything, merely opening the door and letting them precede him down the stairs and then out into the street.

'I had to park my car a little way away,' Stephen said. 'I wasn't too sure where you worked, so I left it a little higher up so that I could explore on foot. You wait here and I'll fetch it. Nice to meet you, sir.' He held out his hand to James, who pretended not to notice, and the minute Stephen was out of earshot she rounded on him.

'Why were you so rude to him? You treated him like a complete idiot! First you turn up here, where I work, knowing that I'd be embarrassed, then as if that wasn't enough, you proceed to make a fool of Stephen!'

'That wasn't altogether difficult,' James drawled, looking down at her. 'Who exactly is he?'

'You *were* introduced,' Claire muttered, taking his question at face value. 'Stephen Hancock. A stockbroker.'

'Yes, yes,' James cut in impatiently, sticking his hands into his pockets and staring at her, 'I know *that*. He made a point of giving me a résumé of himself within the first five minutes of being introduced.'

'Then what's the problem?' she asked innocently. 'You know who he is.'

'Stop playing games with me, dammit.' His voice was curt.

'And stop acting as if you own me! We're over. Remember?'

'Where did you meet him?' he persisted, as if she hadn't spoken, reaching out to curl his fingers around her wrist, and her heart rate accelerated painfully at this physical contact, her body wildly alive.

'At a party,' Claire admitted reluctantly.

'That was fast work,' James murmured, and there was a ferocious undertone to his voice. 'Good catch, is he?'

She raised furious eyes to his. What was it he had said? That he wasn't finished with her yet? That he still wanted her, even if it turned out that she was a gold-digger? She could imagine how he must be feeling now, the great James Forrester who just had to speak softly to be obeyed: he must be thinking that someone else was circling his prey, and he wouldn't be liking that feeling at all.

'I won't even bother to answer that,' she returned, flushing hotly as he swiftly released her wrist to link his fingers through hers, a gesture implicit with threat. 'And *will you let go of me*? Stephen will be here any minute.'

'I don't see what that has to do with my touching you. Are you seeing that boy through some stupid act of defiance? You can't possibly be attracted to him. He's vain and he's quite possibly an opportunist as well.'

'But at least he's not a liar!' she retorted, and his fingers tightened over hers.

'I never lied to you.'

'You just skirted round the truth! Well, it doesn't matter any more.' She carried on with sudden inspiration, 'I happen to find Stephen very attractive, if you must know. He also happens to be entertaining and witty and, yes, a very good catch!'

'You're a fool. He's not your type. He's dangerous.'

'Oh, please, spare me,' she said on a heavy, impatient sigh. 'Next you'll be telling me that you recognise him from Crimewatch.'

His car pulled up to the kerb and she snatched her hand away from James, massaging the blood back into her wrist.

James was looking at the car, his eyes narrowed, debating whether to continue their argument or not.

'Can I go now?' she asked with heavy sarcasm. 'Or are there a few more little insights you'd like to share with me?'

'Oh, you can run along now,' he said lazily, though his eyes were like flint. 'And don't forget to collect your things.'

'Oh, I'll make sure that they're out of your girlfriend's way by the middle of the week.'

She hadn't meant to say that, and she wished that she hadn't when she saw dark amusement flicker in his eyes. He would love to think that she was jealous, she realised, to know that he still had a hold over her, because wasn't that what he wanted: to have her back in that subservient position?

She turned around and walked off towards the car, her body stiff with the awareness that he was watching her.

She had no idea what she talked about for the rest of the evening. Stephen, she recognised vaguely, was charming, but James's appearance had managed to ruin her concentration.

They had dinner at an Italian restaurant in the centre of the town, which was packed even though it was a Monday, and Claire did her utmost to have a good time, laughing in all the right places, asking all the right questions. But her mind was busily playing back that scene with James, lingering over the way her skin had tingled where he had touched her.

It was a relief when they were back at her house. It was becoming difficult to maintain the façade of cheeriness which was the least that Stephen deserved. He had driven out of his way to come and visit her and it would not have been fair to have burdened him with a litany of her own sorry problems. Not that he seemed particularly interested, she thought. He was more interested in finding out about James, his company, his latest expansion into financial consultancy which had been covered in great depth a few weeks before in several of the newspapers.

Claire met these questions blankly, and he laughed at her ignorance, touching her cheek softly so that she jerked back in surprise, then looked apologetically at him. It was hardly a threatening gesture, she told herself with a nervous laugh at her over-reaction. The man wasn't villainous, only a bit egotistic.

She opened her car door and would have slipped out with a little wave and a thank-you, but he detained her before she could do that and asked her when they could meet up again.

'I really don't think it's such a good idea,' Claire said with a frown, not wanting to commit herself.

'You wouldn't want to be responsible for breaking a man's heart, would you?' he asked. 'How about Saturday?'

Claire looked dubiously at his handsome face. It would be silly if she allowed James's warnings to lodge themselves in her head and gnaw away at her. Anyway, he had only said those things in an attempt to put her off Stephen. She smiled, and said, 'Perhaps. Why don't you call me? Just as long as you remember that I'm not looking for any kind of relationship.'

'Of course,' he replied warmly. 'Nor am I!'

She almost expected him to try and kiss her, and she was inordinately relieved when he didn't.

Tony didn't mention a word about either James or Stephen the following day, until she was about to leave when he called her to one side and asked her outright when she would next be seeing James.

'What is he to you, anyway?' he asked, and Claire gave him a withering look. 'OK! So it's none of my business! I just want to find out when you're next seeing him because you could remind him about that little proposition I put to him yesterday when he showed up here.'

'Why should I do your dirty work for you?' she asked, not looking at him, busy clearing her desk. 'Besides, he was only humouring you. He probably has his own network of advertising agencies working for him.'

'You think so?' He gave her an odd look. 'And how is it that you know so much about this guy? I never imagined you as the sort who has a stream of men running around behind you, but if last night was anything to go by...'

He was speculating. She could almost hear his brain whirring away, spinning out explanations, scenarios, feeding that innate curiosity which he felt about everything and everybody. How much longer before the whole office saw her as some sort of femme fatale, which had been the implication behind his words?

'All right,' she snapped, 'I'll mention what you said to him, but don't blame me if nothing comes of it.'

'Good,' Tony beamed at her. 'It's all teamwork, this, and good teamwork is always appreciated.'

This was the first time that she had heard this particular theory being expounded by Tony and she couldn't help but give him a grin of resignation. She could never win with him. He had skin as thick as hide and the sort of brash self-confidence that never got dented.

She went straight to the manor from work, even though she would have preferred to have gone back to the house for a quick shower and a change of clothes. She was rather hoping that James would not be around, despite what he had said to the contrary, in which case she could simply sneak in, take what was hers, and leave. She had managed to borrow Karen's car for the trip so there would be no question of more than one trip needing to be made, while she laboriously hauled whatever it was she had forgotten, off the handlebars of her bike.

She rang the doorbell and was ready to launch into her explanation to the housekeeper for being there when the door was pulled open and she found herself staring at James. He had just had a shower and his hair was still damp and combed back, throwing into relief the sensual curve of his mouth, the straight nose, the aristocratic set of his features.

'I've come to collect my stuff,' she said, cross with herself because of her response to him and resenting him because she was sure that he was there on purpose when normally he would have been in London. 'Shouldn't you still be at work?'

'Is that why you hurried over here so early?' he asked calmly. 'I thought I told you that I would be around when you came. Your things are in the sitting-room.'

Her stuff turned out to be a couple of books, some art supplies which were all but dead and two ancient jumpers which she had forgotten in the tumble drier.

'I could have lived without these,' she informed him. 'I certainly didn't have to rush over here to get them. Your girlfriend could have binned them.'

'My girlfriend?'

'Oh, I'm so sorry,' Claire apologised profusely, 'did I jump to the wrong conclusions? Gayle of the blonde hair, the long legs and the conveniently available location in your cottage, isn't just a friend, is she? Silly me, I just assumed...'

'Jealous?' James asked, raising his eyebrows in a question.

'Disappointed,' she returned without blinking. 'I suppose I vainly thought that there might be a little breathing space between myself and my replacement.'

His mouth tightened and he took a step towards her. Her breathing quickened and she had to fight not to show him how desperately aware she was of him, attuned to his every movement, to the way his dark hair sprang back from his forehead, the green eyes fringed with thick, black, almost feminine lashes, the strong arms and long, clever fingers. Everything about him radiated an energy that sapped her of her fragile will power.

'Gayle and I go back a long way,' he said softly and she laughed, feeling tears prick the back of her eyes.

'So she told me. Old friends. Or whatever.'

He walked slowly towards her, with that lazy, graceful ease of movement that always made her think of something stealthy, untamed, and a thousand drums began beating in her head, against her temples, sending her nerves into chaotic tension.

What did he think he was doing, cornering her like this? Confusing her? She felt like a trapped animal, on the verge of escape but mesmerised by the hunter. She could hardly breathe.

He stood in front of her, inches away, and the clean male scent of him went to her head like incense.

She heard herself stammering that she really had to leave and she wanted to scream in frustration at what he could still do to her.

'Nervous, Claire?' he asked softly. 'Why?'

'I am not nervous!' she shot back, but her hands were tightly clutching her bag and her legs felt like jelly.

'There's no need to be,' he murmured smoothly, as if she hadn't spoken. 'Aren't you forgetting how well we know each other?' He managed to invest that simple statement with a degree of eroticism that made her break out in a fine film of perspiration.

Every pore in her body was aching to be touched by him. Her breasts felt heavy, her nipples hard and erect. She wanted him so badly, and it was made worse by the fact that she could remember only too vividly what it was like to feel his hands on her, exploring every inch of her.

'I must go,' she flung out wildly and she turned around, but she hadn't made it halfway across the room when she heard his voice behind her like a whip.

'I'm not finished with you.'

'Dear me,' she returned angrily, facing him across the room like a sparring partner, 'how unfortunate, considering I'm finished with *you*!'

He glared at her, his mouth hostile, his dark brows drawn in angry frown, and she didn't know whether to laugh at the way she had managed to get under his skin with her coolness, or run for her life before he demolished it completely and left her defenceless.

'That'll be the day,' he snarled, approaching her in two easy strides. He entwined his fingers in her hair, and she realised with shock that they were both breathing quickly. There was a dangerous excitement in the air and it frightened her, because it could eat her up and spit her out and she wouldn't be able to do a thing about it.

She wriggled against him, but that only made things worse. It only brought them into even closer physical contact.

'Let me go!' she demanded, hearing the pleading tone in her voice with a mixture of dismay and disgust.

'Why?' he mocked, his lips thinning. 'Have you got an appointment?'

'With Stephen!' she threw at him rashly.

'Wrong response, darling.'

It was the last thing he said before his lips claimed hers.

CHAPTER SEVEN

FOR the briefest time Claire was suspended in air, her body ablaze with sensation, tasting his mouth against hers with helpless surrender. Her head was flung back, her eyes half closed, and his hand was curved around her neck. She could feel her pulse beating against his fingers. He nipped her full lower lip with his teeth and she moaned convulsively. Everything, every movement, every caress seemed to happen in slow motion, as though it was all lasting an eternity when in fact, it was only a matter of seconds, then she sprang back from him trembling violently.

She didn't know what to say, where to look. So much, she thought bitterly, for my grand mastery of self-control. She had managed, at least, to salvage some bit of self-respect by pulling away from him before it all got totally and humiliatingly out of hand. Big deal. It was as plain as day that she was still acutely aroused by him. It was visible, she knew, in the hot flush on her cheeks, in her swollen lips, and in her fast, uneven breathing. If he had wanted to prove a point, then he had done so, hands down.

She turned away, and he pulled her back to face him, his eyes icy.

'So you're hurrying off to Stephen,' he bit out in a cold voice. 'After your response to me just then, I'd be surprised if you had anything left for the boy.'

'Oh, you would, would you?' was all she could find to say, which seemed thoroughly ineffectual.

'Have you slept with him?' he demanded savagely, then he swept on without waiting for an answer, which was just as well since she couldn't think of one. 'You're a fool, a complete idiot. What do you think you're playing at, running around with him? You're like chalk and cheese. Don't you think I don't know how gullible you are underneath all that new-found self-possession?'

'Stop preaching to me! I can run my life very nicely on my own, thank you very much!'

'No, you can't. If you could, you wouldn't be seeing that twerp.'

Her eyes darkened at his tone of voice. 'And I suppose I was in safe hands when I was with you?' she asked, and a dull flush crept into his cheeks.

'At least I looked after you.'

'Ha! Don't make me laugh. You looked after yourself. You slept with me because you fancied me, except you never let it really get to you, did you? You've locked your emotions away in an ivory tower—no, in the same coffin as your wife!' She stopped, appalled at her lack of sensitivity, expecting his roar of anger at her presumption.

'I'm sorry,' she whispered.

He appeared to have turned to stone and she reached out to tentatively touch his face, starting as his hand snapped out and his fingers gripped her wrist.

'I should damn well leave you to get on with your mistakes,' he bit out and she glared at him, stoked to anger by that remark. Of all the high-handed, arrogant, *typical* remarks, that took the biscuit. Next, she thought, he'll be telling me that I should be grateful for him ruining my life! You wouldn't catch him dead treating Gayle just-good-friends King like a complete halfwit, she thought stormily. And had he treated his wife like that? she wanted to know. Ha!

'I wish you would!'

'What's the real reason behind you seeing him? Has he promised you money? Marriage? Is that it?'

'Money? Marriage? What are you on about? I barely know the man!'

'Well, it can't be attraction.'

'Why not?' Her eyes flashed. 'He happens to be extremely good-looking.'

'If you happen to like the plastic look.'

'Maybe I do! Maybe it comes as quite a nice change from you!'

He looked at her in disbelief and for an alarming second she thought that he was going to kiss her again, to prove irrevocably that her feelings, at least on a physical basis, were reserved for him alone. On some wild impulse, she said recklessly, 'It's none of your business, but I'm very interested in him! And turned on! You're not the only man capable of arousing me, you know.'

His eyes were black with fury but it was too late to retract the lie, and besides, why should she? It was her life, and she could do just as she wanted with it, whether James Forrester liked it or not! If she wanted to sleep with a million men, then who was he to have any say in the matter?

Her biggest mistake had been letting him know from the beginning how she felt about him. He could be shrewdly manipulative in his dealings with people, and by declaring her love for him, like a fool, she had played right into his hands.

'You wouldn't be so damned aroused if you knew what sort of reputation he had,' James said grimly, and her eyes widened in surprise.

'What are you talking about?' she asked, bewildered. 'Reputation? What reputation?'

'I asked Gayle about your Stephen Hancock and what she told me doesn't make pleasant reading.'

Claire's jaw dropped and she stared at him, outraged. 'You spied on him?'

'I didn't *spy* on him,' he returned, not meeting her eyes. 'But he did mention where he worked, and, as Gayle used to work there, I thought I'd ask her whether she had ever heard of him, just out of interest.'

'*Just out of interest*? You never do anything *just out of interest*! There's always an ulterior motive with you. How could you? What else did you tell her? Did you tell her about us? Did you have a good laugh at my expense?'

'Don't be dramatic.' He turned away, his mouth tight, and she followed him to the sofa, where he sat down heavily, leaning back to look at her from under his lashes, his hands clasped behind his head.

He looked totally relaxed and she could have killed him. Who did he think he was, asking questions behind her back? She stood staring down at him, her hands on her hips, her eyes blazing.

'I am not being dramatic!' she yelled. 'And anyway, what if I were? Wouldn't you be dramatic if someone decided to spy on one of your friends?'

'Don't you want to know what I found out?'

'No, I do not want to know what you found out.'

She turned away and eyed the door. She should walk out of here, take her belongings and leave, that's what she ought to do. Let him keep his precious information to himself; she wasn't interested in hearing gossip anyway, was she?

'What did you find out?' she asked, glaring at him.

'Sit down,' he replied. 'You're looming, and it's putting me off my stride.'

'Nothing puts you off your stride,' Claire muttered and he gave her a wicked smile. He could change from fury to charm at the drop of a hat, and right now she wished that he'd just stick to the fury. James Forrester in a charming mood was dangerous. She sat down primly, her hands on her knees, leaning forward so that her hair swung against her cheeks. 'You shouldn't have asked questions about Stephen behind my back,' she said accusingly, before he started giving her any spiel about being grateful to him for his revelations.

'Why not?' he asked bluntly.

'Because we're friends, and you don't give a damn about me, so I can't see why you should be interested in my welfare.'

He looked at her thoughtfully, stroking his chin, then he said, 'The man's a philanderer. Apparently he's got quite a reputation at Carter's. Gayle doesn't personally know him, she left before he joined, but she's kept in touch with quite a few people from there, and they all say the same thing: that he's unscrupulous.'

She had more or less suspected what he was going to tell her; after all, he was hardly likely to inform her that rumour had it that Stephen was a boy wonder and as wholesome as apple pie. Nevertheless, it annoyed and hurt her to think that he considered her so innocent that she needed warning because she couldn't take care of herself.

'So,' she said in a saccharine voice, 'in other words, all this is from a friend of a friend.'

The lazy charm vanished as quickly as it had appeared and his brows met in an angry frown.

'I can assure you that Gayle isn't one to lie.'

'No,' Claire retorted, 'well, she wouldn't be, would she?'

'And what the hell is that supposed to mean?'

'You've chosen to like her,' she said sarcastically, 'so that must mean that her credentials are pristine. I dare say that apart from looking like she's just stepped off a magazine cover, and being brainy with it, she's probably queueing up for sainthood.' That sounded so horribly jealous that she carried on quickly, 'Anyway, thanks for the word of warning. I'll try and remember it.'

She stood up and he roared at her, 'Sit back down!'

'I will not! I'm going home. And there's no need to show me to the door—I know where it is.'

She walked away defiantly and, as she pulled open the door, it was slammed back shut and he kept his hand there, outstretched, making sure that she couldn't leave.

She found that she couldn't look at him, not in the eyes. He was too close for that. His proximity addled her wits and she stubbornly shifted her eyes to the huge French doors behind him.

'You will not see him again.'

'Excuse me?'

'You heard me,' he rasped. 'You wouldn't stand a chance with a man like that, and there's no point in holding your head up high and pretending to be immune to what I'm telling you. I know you better than you think. No, if you want to walk out on what we have, then that's your right, but you're to steer well clear of that man. He's no good.'

'If I wanted you to run my life for me,' she said tightly, 'I would have asked. In the meantime, feel free to assume that I can run my life by myself.'

'I'd need to see that to believe it.'

She still wasn't looking at him but she could feel his eyes boring into her, probing to depths which only he could reach.

'Why are you doing this?' she asked in a low, panicked voice.

'Because you haven't got a clue about handling a man like Hancock. He cultivates women, he's been known to accept presents from them. From what I've heard, he probably sees it as his right. You might not be able to afford to give him presents, but, from what I've heard and the little I've seen of him, you're the sort to intrigue him. He's a barracuda looking for something tasty and innocent to devour.'

'He's nothing like that!' she protested, and he shook his head impatiently, catching her chin with his fingers and forcing her to look at him, which she did, reluctantly.

'Listen to what I'm saying,' he threw out, his face dark with restless anger. 'Don't be stupid. Don't go out with that man simply because you've become disillusioned with me.'

'And don't be so damned conceited!' She hated the way he could see into her. How could she be expected to protect herself when it was so easy for him to break down her defences? 'I'll see whoever I choose to, and now would you mind removing your hand from the door?'

He stepped back and shoved his hands into his pockets, and she could see that he was debating whether he should continue on his course of persuasion. She knew him well enough to realise that her obstinacy would have infuriated him, but she had no intention of bowing and scraping and thanking him for interfering in her life. He must really, she thought, have absolutely no respect for my intelligence, if he thinks that he has to jump in and warn me off Stephen Hancock.

No wonder their relationship had come to nothing. Even without the shadow of his wife dictating its outcome, she wouldn't have been of marriageable quality for him anyway. Fine to fool around with, but it was obvious that he liked them brainy and it was equally obvious that he considered her to be about as brainy as a baked potato.

'And stay out of my life,' she said, her fingers on the door handle.

'Or else what?' he asked tightly. 'What will you do? Go on, tell me, I'm dying to know.'

She didn't answer that. Instead, she walked out of the room, her back straight and her head held high, half expecting him to follow her out and pick up the pieces of his argument.

It was a relief when she made it to the front door and she practically ran to the car, fumbling with the lock and tossing her bag of stuff on to the back seat, then she spun round in the courtyard, reversing the little car as if the devil was on her tail, and accelerated down the long tree-lined drive, passing the cottage and scowling at it.

Gayle King, indeed. Oh, Gayle King said this, and Gayle King said that. Had Gayle King also clicked her tongue and shaken her head sadly and told him that he ought to warn her off Stephen Hancock? Claire thought sourly. No. James would never listen and obey anything anyone said unless he happened to agree personally with their opinion. No, he had taken it upon himself to preach to her about the folly of becoming involved with Stephen because he ranked her as a total idiot when it came to handling members of the opposite sex.

Oh, why had she ever thrown herself at him? she wondered miserably. How smug and self-satisfied he must have felt, warning her off. He still wanted her, and in the absence of her compliance with this, what better than to make sure that the competition was eliminated?

He wouldn't have fabricated what he had told her about Stephen, she reflected, as she later lay in bed, staring upwards at the ceiling, but had he embellished what was basically hearsay? It certainly would have suited his purpose, and who knew what pleasure he derived from watching her face when he told her about Stephen. She had tried to school her features into an impassive, unreadable mask, but she was new at such games and no doubt he saw right through them to the confused, dismayed girl underneath.

Whether she believed what he had said or not, though, it was food for thought, and when Stephen did call on Saturday to invite her up to London to see a play she made some polite excuse and declined the invitation.

'You sound different,' he said suspiciously down the phone. 'What's the matter, babe? I was hoping you'd be my guide around this lovely city of yours.'

'I'd be a hopeless guide,' Claire said. 'I hardly know London at all. I can recommend a few good agents, though.'

'None as enchanting as you,' he murmured huskily, and she frowned at the charcoals lying on her desk.

'Look, I'm not interested in flirting, Stephen,' she said brusquely. 'I thought I had made that absolutely clear when we met at my sister's party.'

'I'm not flirting,' he countered in such a sober, reasonable voice that she wondered whether her imagination had been playing tricks on her. 'It's just that I'm thousands of miles away from my home, away from friends. I'm sorry if I came on too strong, but it was just nice to meet someone I feel I can relate to.'

She relaxed slightly. 'Fine,' she said, feeling much better now she had informed him where he stood, which was nowhere, 'but I still can't make it tonight. I've got other plans.'

'What about tomorrow?' he asked swiftly, and she found herself being talked into dinner at one of the more expensive London restaurants.

Am I being stupid? she asked herself afterwards. She had not given him the slightest reason to think that she was willing to sleep with him, and if he enjoyed her company then what was the harm in the occasional meal out? It wasn't as though he was going to be in London indefinitely. And it was more therapeutic than staying indoors or going out with her girlfriends, who were only interested in going to parties. Karen was different, but, even so, she couldn't rely on her for a social life.

And anyway, she thought defiantly, Stephen could be quite amusing sometimes. Then she had to laugh at the way she was justifying her actions to herself. I'm a big girl now, she told herself, despite what James Forrester cares to think, and I can take care of myself as good as the next person.

Sitting in the ultra-expensive, ultra-sophisticated London restaurant the following evening, she almost wished that James was around so that he could see just how capably she was handling herself.

She had worn a very simple but very flattering olive-green dress which looked like linen but wasn't, a pair of flat gold sandals and some muted gold jewellery. Nothing ostentatious, nothing that would give a man the wrong idea, and she had made sure that the conversation remained on a purely impersonal level, which, as it turned out, brought out the most amusing side of Stephen. He had travelled quite a bit and some of his stories, when he didn't play a starring role, were very funny.

He was dressed expensively but not flamboyantly and she tried to match him with the opportunist painted by James, the man who accepted gifts from women, presumably in return for services rendered. Had that been an imaginative touch on James's part? she asked herself. Surely someone like that would be more—well, more vulgar? Gold medallions perhaps; a bracelet, a few rings.

She should, she knew, have asked him, in a roundabout manner, about what Gayle had said about him, but in the end she didn't. It was no business what he did with himself in New York. He could surround himself with a harem of women for all she cared, just so long as he obeyed her hands-off message to him. Anyway, she resented her private life being discussed by James Forrester and his lady-friend. To have quizzed Stephen on what he did or didn't do behind closed doors would have been tantamount to being grateful for James's interference.

They enjoyed dinner in an atmosphere of relative amicability. No innuendoes from Stephen, no lingering looks, nothing to suggest that he was an unpleasant, cleverly camouflaged Don Juan angling for a romp in the hay.

By the time they were strolling through Leicester Square in search of a taxi to take her to the station she felt completely at ease, and all the more so when he informed her, ruefully, that his time in England was up.

'Already?' Claire asked, surprised. 'I thought you were here for two months.' She couldn't say that there wasn't a touch of relief in her response to this bit of news, but he didn't seem to notice it. He was shaking his head, glancing at her sideways.

'So,' he said with overdone gloom, 'did I. But the powers that be have decided otherwise. Apparently there's some urgent business that I've specifically been asked to do on behalf of a client, so I'm being flown back over.'

'Still,' Claire said, 'you'll be glad to get back to your friends.'

'Not so glad to leave others behind,' he replied ambiguously, and she gave him a vague, uncomprehending smile.

The taxi was pulling up, something of a miracle at this hour in Central London, and she held out her hand politely.

'Well, thank you for the meals. It's been fun. Maybe the next time you're in London you can look me up and we can get together for a laugh.'

'Not so fast,' he murmured smoothly, folding his hand over hers and smiling. 'I don't leave for another week and a half. Time enough for one or two more meals, wouldn't you say?'

Claire laughed and was saved from saying anything by the taxi driver who had shoved open the passenger door and was leaning across to bellow something about having better things to do than hang about for hours while they gassed.

'You either hop in, luv, or else I'm off.'

'I'm in!' Claire said, turning away as Stephen leaned forward to kiss her. She politely proffered her cheek, but his head dipped down and his lips touched hers. There was nothing searching or urgent in the kiss, but still the gesture took her so much by surprise that she could only stare at him for a few seconds, red-faced and disturbed. She didn't know whether she should ignore that or else rebuff him, but in any event she was spared from doing either by the taxi driver, who was accelerating meaningfully.

By the following morning she had put the uncomfortable episode to the back of her mind.

She was the last to arrive at work for once. She had overslept and had had to condense her usual forty-minute routine of shower, clothes and breakfast into a rushed fifteen minutes. The breakfast had had to be eliminated, and as a result she arrived at the office ravenously hungry.

She stopped off at the office kitchen, a must as far as Tony was concerned because coffee machines, he assured them all, were bad for the health, and poured herself a strong cup of black percolated coffee, complete with two heaping teaspoons of sugar. It wasn't as good as a bowl of cereal, but it would have to do, and she hurried to her desk, only to be halted in mid-stride by Tony, who had stuck his head out of his office and was gesticulating for her.

Why is this always such a madhouse? Claire thought, dumping her bag on the desk and grimacing at Karen who was stopped as she leaned across to whisper something by Tony snapping shut the door behind him and striding towards her.

'All right, all right! I'm coming!'

He walked back towards his office and Claire followed in his wake, clutching her cup of coffee. Couldn't he have at least allowed her to enjoy her first cup of coffee for the morning? As she walked into his office, she opened her mouth to tell him about as much and then shut it just as quickly, freezing to the spot just inside the doorway and staring at James with mounting horror.

He was dressed for work in an immaculately cut grey suit which made Tony's trendier oatmeal-coloured linen one appear garish in comparison. His legs were crossed and the green eyes were fixed on her with irony.

'Well,' Tony hustled her in from behind the desk, 'close the door, will you? What time do you call this? I told Mr Forrester that you were always the first in.' He turned to James with a winning smile, 'After myself, at least.'

Claire had to tear her eyes away from James. It was a shock seeing him here, lean and dark and vital and in apparently no rush to leave. What was he doing? It wasn't a social visit, so it must be to do with business, which would go a long way to explaining Tony's syco-phantic behaviour, but why then had *she* been summoned?

'Sit down, sit down,' Tony was saying, gesturing to the chair next to James's, and Claire frowned at it.

'Must I?'

Tony ignored that, but out of the corner of her eye Claire could see James's lazy acknowledgement at the remark.

'Hello, Claire,' he said in a deep, cool voice, reaching out, and Claire looked at his extended hand, appalled.

'Hi,' she mumbled, making the polite gesture as brief as possible, but still feeling the thrill of electricity at the physical contact. She sat down, cross to find that her legs were shaky, and kept her eyes pointedly averted from James. She could feel him staring at her from under those thick lashes, though, one hand casually resting on his thigh, the other on the armrest of the swivel-chair. He made everything in the office seem a little overdone and ever so slightly tacky. The furnishings, she knew, had been purchased on the cheap, when Tony had first been doing up the office, because he hadn't been able to afford anything much better. Since then, he had gradually been replacing things bit by bit, trading in his small, rigid chair for something a bit better and more comfortable, then upgrading the desks in the main office one by one. With time, she had become too accustomed to her surroundings to pay much attention to them, but now she realised for the first time how seriously some of it was in need of redecoration.

'How are you?' James asked, and she was forced to face him, if only out of politeness.

'Fine,' she muttered briefly.

'Done anything interesting since I last saw you?' he asked in a deeply courteous voice. 'I believe when we last met we were surprised to find that a certain acquaintance was known to us both?'

Tony was smiling approvingly at this little interchange. He liked this rapport between them. Somehow he thought that it cast a pleasant reflection on him.

'Did we?' Claire asked, wide-eyed. 'I can't recall.' She turned her attention back to Tony, who was choosing to ignore her. He was looking at James, offering him another top-up of coffee, which she was glad to hear declined because the last thing she intended doing was scurrying out to the kitchen to pour a cup of coffee for James Forrester.

'I guess we should just get down to business straight away,' Tony said in a voice that made her want to grind her teeth with helpless frustration. 'I understand that time is money for you.' He laughed at that and then directed a frown at her. 'We could have started half an hour ago if you had shown up on time.'

'I did show up on time,' Claire said mildly. 'My working hours are...'

'Yes, yes, yes, well, you're here now and we can get on with it.'

'You could have started without me, I'm sure,' she pointed out icily, more for James's benefit than for Tony's. In other words, she intended to make clear to him, I don't want to be here, and he read her intonation without batting an eyelid.

'On the contrary,' he drawled smoothly from next to her, 'you're an integral part of my proposition.'

'I see,' she muttered, feverishly trying to work out what was going on. He was playing some kind of game. Not content to have thoroughly ruined her life, not content to have spied on Stephen with whom she might well have decided to have an affair for all he knew, he was now further turning the screw by embroiling her in some stupid scheme which would probably involve her being humiliated even more. Couldn't he just leave her alone? Was this his way of getting his own back for her having the temerity to walk out on him? By coming here, he had put her in a position of impotence. What could she do? Risk her career by standing up and refusing to deal with him? Throw a fit and accuse him of taking advantage of his power by leading poor Tony up the garden path? Hardly. No, all she could do was sit here and grit her teeth, which he would find very amusing.

'And what is your proposition?' she asked with no attempt at curiosity, and was treated to a black frown from Tony.

'Over to you,' he said, nodding briefly to Tony, who beamed like a well-fed cat.

'A marvellous deal,' he said on cue. 'Mr Forrester——'

'James, please, if we're to be doing business together.'

'James,' he said obligingly, as if he had been granted a miracle. 'James has offered us a huge advertising contract for one of his bigger subsidiaries. Billboards, magazines, newspapers, the lot.'

'Really?' Claire said. 'How interesting.' How unbelievable, her voice implied.

'I don't think you realise what an opportunity this is,' Tony said warningly. 'Perhaps I can have a word with you outside, Claire?'

'Perhaps,' James interrupted, 'I could have the word with her instead? Why don't you get us some coffees?'

Claire grinned reluctantly to herself. Tony would hate that. Getting coffees? It was tantamount to asking him if he wouldn't mind parading down the High Street in the nude, but of course he was as trapped as she was, incapable of doing anything but obeying because James Forrester was not only a potential client, but far and away the most important one his little company had ever had. Normally he dealt with small firms, quite a few of them family-owned. This, he knew, could put him in the big time, and he wasn't about to jeopardise that by arguing the toss over fetching a few coffees. He stood up and looked at Claire, who shook her head, and then left the office dutifully.

'Your boss isn't very impressed with you,' James said, as soon as the door had shut behind him, and her teeth met angrily.

'What are you doing here?'

'I thought it was obvious. Bringing some big business in for Tony.'

'Why won't you leave me alone?'

'The contract could be worth a lot of money,' he said, as if she hadn't spoken. 'And look at me when I'm talking to you.'

'Or else what?' she asked, looking at him.

'That better. I hate talking to a shoulder. Have you seen Stephen—that's his name, isn't it?—since we last spoke?'

'Yes, not that it's any of your business.' Now that she was facing him, she found that she couldn't keep her eyes away. It was like a starving man who had been shown a plateful of food, piping hot, ready to be eaten. She took in everything, the easy incline of his body in the chair, the hard set of his features, the sensuous curve of his mouth, the sardonic stare of those amazing eyes.

'And did you mention the sort of reputation he has in New York?'

'I did not! Anyway, it doesn't matter; he leaves London in a few days' time.'

'Does he?' He lowered his eyes, then looked at her. 'And how do you feel about that? A wasted opportunity?'

'Don't be so insulting. I can't believe you bamboozled your way into this office, leading poor Tony up the garden path with some fairy-story about contracts, just to corner me.'

He gave her a look that implied that she was mad and she glared at him.

'And don't give me that innocent look,' she said.

'All sparks, aren't you?' was his only comment. 'A far cry from that obliging girl who——'

'That was a long time ago!' Claire cut in, going scarlet. 'You're not being fair on Tony. He really believes you. He's on Cloud Nine. How do you think he's going to feel when you tell him that we won't be doing the advertising? No billboards, no magazines, no newspapers, nothing. I know you have your own advertising contacts.'

'Which have been eliminated. They weren't doing their job.' He shrugged one elegant shoulder and her eyes widened.

There was a hesitant knock on the door and Tony entered, carrying two cups of coffee on a tray, along with some biscuits which he had respectfully placed on a small flowery saucer.

Wow, she thought, biscuits! He really was going all-out. She glanced across at James, who gave her a dry, comprehending look, and she looked away, unhinged by that flash of telepathic understanding that had sparked between them. How could she have forgotten that intuitive empathy they had shared?

'Has Mr Forrester—James—explained what he wants?' Tony asked, sitting back down after James had accepted the cup of coffee and declined the biscuits. Claire noticed that she hadn't been offered a biscuit, an unconscious oversight on Tony's part, which was a shame since her stomach was beginning to rumble with hunger.

'I haven't given her any details,' James said smoothly. 'I thought that I'd leave that to you. You can give her the technical info far better than I could.'

Tony puffed up at that and obediently launched into what the deal would involve and where she would fit in.

'And the best part of it,' he ended by saying, with a huge, satisfied grin on his face, 'for you at any rate, is that you'll be the one going along with James to work on the details. It'll mean a week or so out of the office, but that's no problem.'

It took a moment for what Tony had said to sink in, then she sat up in her chair, startled.

'Go along...? With...?'

'Me...' James filled in drily. 'To Paris. My secretary has already worked out the details.'

Tony was beaming. His grin was so wide that at any minute she suspected that his face would crack in two. She wasn't grinning, though. She sat there, feeling cornered.

'I can't just drop everything that I'm doing...' she protested a little desperately.

'Permission granted,' Tony grinned. 'Besides, you're nearly through with that bicycle advert, aren't you?'

She nodded despairingly and he inclined his head as if to say, Well, that's all right, then.

'You leave the day after tomorrow,' he informed her expansively, while James surveyed her calmly and in silence. 'I trust you have no further objections?'

'I may have other plans,' she protested weakly, and he shot her a dark look.

'Of course,' Tony continued, all business now, 'I dare say you'll need a slightly different wardrobe from the one you're accustomed to wearing to work.'

Claire looked down at her trousers and short-sleeved shirt. She never wore anything expensive or dressy to work, not in her job, which was just as well since she possessed precious few things along those lines anyway.

'This is all I have,' she said with a certain amount of satisfaction. 'Perhaps someone more suitable could take my place.'

'Nonsense.' The cool dry voice killed off that idea. 'Buy yourself a few things. Add it to the overall bill.' He stood up and Tony hastily followed suit.

'Fine,' she said, glancing at Tony who was rummaging on his desk for his fountain pen. 'Any more orders?' she hissed at James and he smiled lazily.

'None that I can think of. For the moment.'

CHAPTER EIGHT

CLAIRE had no idea how she was going to sort out this one. She was sensible enough to realise that there was no way that she could wriggle out of Paris. Someone with a bit more nerve and a much greater talent for lying might have been able to feign a broken leg, or a fractured arm or Asian flu, but she had never been a good liar, and this was not a time to try and find out if her capabilities in that area had improved.

Anyway, even if she really did come down with something, James Forrester was not the sort to be easily put off. She knew him too well for that. He was tenacious. Once he had decided on a course of action, he would never drop it. She had once admired that trait of his, finding in it an element of strength which had been lacking in most of the men she had met throughout her life. Now, though, that admiration seemed a little misplaced.

It was only later, when Stephen called her at the house, that she discovered the one and only benefit to Paris.

'I'm sorry,' she said with genuine warmth fuelled by relief at the fact that she wasn't having to lie or evade. 'I can't see you before you go back to America, Stephen. I've been given a job which will involve my being out of the country.'

He sounded incredulous. 'You've been given a job abroad? Is Fate working against us?' He laughed at his quip and she made a polite noise which she hoped sounded like sympathy. 'Where are you going?' he asked.

'Paris. I leave the day after tomorrow, in fact. Just time enough to dash into Reading tomorrow for a few essentials.'

'Paris.' He sounded envious. 'Nice. I've been to gay Paree a couple of times myself. On business, of course, so I never managed to make it to the tourist spots. Where will you be staying?'

She hesitated fractionally, then gave him the name of the hotel, one of the most expensive, and he whistled under his breath.

'Rich client,' he said, and she grunted in agreement.

'Well,' she murmured apologetically, 'thanks for the meals while you've been here and have a good trip back to New York.'

'Sure, babe,' he said, but he sounded a little cool and she shrugged her shoulders. He had no reason to be cold. She wasn't putting him off, because there was nothing *to* put off. They had had a few meals together and that was all.

It was an odd relief to think that she wouldn't be seeing him again. James and his revelations must have got to me more than I like to think, she mused, running a bath and settling into it with abandon.

Suspicion was a curious thing, she thought. Once the seeds of it were strategically sown, they took root and there was nothing you could do to eradicate them. And James had sown those seeds of suspicion the minute he had told her about Stephen's reputation.

She raced through the shops the following morning, one eye on her watch, the other on getting together some kind of wardrobe that would look businesslike. Pride stopped her from buying anything too expensive, but common sense dictated that she not waste James's money on absolute rock-bottom rubbish that would probably fall to bits after a few wearings.

Karen had been green with envy when Claire had told her where she would be over the coming week.

'Paris. Desperately romantic,' she had said with a faraway look, and Claire had made a face.

'I don't think so. It's business.'

'Business? Hah. Romantic with a capital R. Especially with that gorgeous hunk of a man whom, incidentally, I would kill for.'

Karen had been good about not asking her any questions about what exactly had gone on between James and her, but Claire knew that she must have been curious. Who wouldn't have been? One minute she was happily ensconced in an idyllic cottage in the grounds of Frilton Manor, the next minute she was looking for alternative accommodation and clearing out as if the hounds of hell were on her tail.

'He must be in love with you,' she had said, and Claire had responded bitterly,

'Hardly.' Determined, she thought, suspicious, cynical, emotionally unreachable, but definitely not in love. She had firmly changed the subject and that had been the end of that, but as she rushed through the shops she knew, irritably, that she was choosing clothes that James would like. The oatmeal-coloured lightweight suit, with its fitted skirt and flattering jacket, which made her look older and more sophisticated than she would have believed possible. The black trousers, cuffed at the ankles, and of a soft material that felt like silk against her skin. The two gorgeous blouses in apricot and turquoise. She packed her suitcase hurriedly, and it was only when she had finished that she realised that she had omitted most of her comfortable, well-worn, unbecoming outfits. Things which had been with her for more years than she cared to mention, and, as her sister had said more than once, had long ago passed their sell-by date. As an afterthought, she had thrown in the adventurous little number which had caused such a sensation at her sister's party, which, she thought, was silly, because she doubted that there would be an opportunity to bring it out, and even if there were such an opportunity, she had no intention of bringing it out. Knowing the way that James's complicated if not downright convoluted mind worked, he would probably think that she was ready and willing to hop back into bed with him. In fact, she thought dubiously, he would probably think that she had spent hours hunting down clothes to impress him, and on that thought she very nearly unpacked the suitcase and replaced all her new purchases with her regular standbys. It was only the fact that she would be called upon to make some kind of impression on other people that stopped her.

Then she became even more annoyed and flustered that she was debating the issue anyway. She wouldn't have been, if it had concerned anyone other than James. The fact was that she wanted to appear aloof and cool, but under the surface the same pull was always there, the same urge to feel his eyes on her, even though a part of her sensibly told her that she wanted no more to do with him.

She wanted to drive him crazy even while she desperately longed to be able to turn her back on him with the same cool self-possession which she forced herself to display whenever she was in his presence.

It was the constant warring of fire and ice that was driving her mad. She hated him with every bone in her body for having desired her, when what she wanted was his love, but then his desire could still send the adrenalin rushing through her, making her heady and uncontrolled.

How was she going to stand being in his company for eight days? Eight minutes was bad enough. She tried to console herself with the thought that she could always explore Paris on her own in the evenings, a particularly unalluring thought, and of course there would be people around them during the day, so maybe things wouldn't be too bad.

They were to meet at Heathrow Airport at a pre-arranged time, and she spotted him as soon as she arrived the following morning.

He was standing with his back to her, and she stopped in her tracks for a few seconds, absorbing him, the smooth, lean lines of his body, the hint of power visible from the confident way he carried himself.

He was talking to one of the girls behind the checking-in desk. Claire looked at the rapt expression on her face and felt a sharp pang of jealousy, which she shakily reminded herself wasn't going to do at all. She couldn't afford to begin to let him see how vulnerable she still was with him. He must guess, of course, but she knew that if she succeeded in maintaining a remote exterior he would not be sure, not one hundred per cent at any rate. His instinct would tell him that she was still crazy about him, after all she had spent months openly confessing her love, but his head would put him on shaky ground, which was exactly what she wanted. He might question whether her love hadn't been girlish infatuation, something which had become tarnished at the edges since she had left.

She walked up briskly behind him and said hello, more or less ignoring his presence and handing over her ticket to the girl who took it with a reluctant sigh at the abrupt end to her conversation with him.

James turned to her, and she felt the full force of his green stare on her, in response to which she produced an efficient smile which she flashed at him and which met with a look of dry irony.

'I see you took me at my word, about the clothes,' he murmured mildly. 'There was no need to dress quite so stylishly for the flight over.'

The girl handed over the ticket and boarding pass, and they walked off, with Claire keeping some safe distance between them.

'I'm here on business,' she pointed out. 'I agree with you that I have to dress the part. It's one thing to sit in front of a draughting table in jeans and a sweatshirt, but I wouldn't dream of trying to win an account in the same dress.'

'Well,' James drawled, 'you look delightful, if a little on the old side.'

'Thank you,' Claire responded tartly. 'You always were one to be blunt.'

'I believe there was a time when you rather liked that trait in me.'

She still did, but she wasn't going to admit that now, so she didn't say anything, and they spent the rest of the time at the airport in silence, a companionable silence, interrupted only by harmless small talk which she felt she could cope with easily enough.

Some of the carefully imposed self-control deserted her as the plane landed at Charles de Gaulle Airport in Paris, and she leant forward in her seat, enthusiastically looking out of the window. She had never been to Paris before. It had always been one of those places which she had intended to visit, just as soon as she saved enough money to do it in relative comfort, but had somehow never got around to it. James had asked her to accompany him on some of his business trips, but a part of her had always baulked at the thought of being taken there as a rich man's escort, even though she knew that he would have been furious if he had discovered that that was her line of thinking. Or maybe, she now thought, it would just have been in keeping with what he thought of her as a gold-digger. Those remarks of his had hit home with her. They had stuck like mud, and, however much she told herself that of course he didn't really think that of her, she couldn't be sure.

Now he said lazily, reading her mind, 'We could have come here together sooner.'

'I never seemed to have the money readily available,' she replied, her body twisted away from him.

'I wouldn't have proposed that we travelled Dutch,' he said, with a frown in his voice.

'No, but I would have.'

'Has anyone ever told you that you're too damned proud for your own good? Don't you know the cliché that pride comes before a fall?'

'You should know all about pride,' Claire muttered, turning towards him, her cheeks bright red. 'That's why I'm here, isn't it? Because I dented your pride when I walked out on you, and you're determined to rescue it by proving that you can seduce me back into bed with you?'

His brows met in an angry frown. 'I don't have to prove anything to anyone,' he said tautly.

'Who are you trying to kid? I know you, James Forrester. I know how your mind works.'

'And I know you. I know that whatever you say, you're still attracted to me, despite the fact that you've pulled that twerp out of a closet somewhere. A piece of massive misjudgement, might I add.'

For a second he lost her, then she realised that he was talking about Stephen. His face was charged with angry emotion, then he lowered his eyes and said softly, 'But of course, that little problem has been sorted out, hasn't it?'

Claire looked at him in astonishment. 'Sorted out? How so? Explain yourself.'

He shrugged and looked oddly uncomfortable for a fraction of a second. 'Well, as you said, he isn't going to be around when you get back, is he?'

'Why am I suddenly suspicious?' She forgot about staring through the window and concentrated her attention on James's face instead.

'I have no idea. Why are you? Perhaps it's in your nature.'

'You didn't have anything to do with Stephen's sudden need to leave London, did you?' she asked and was met with a thick silence. 'No, you wouldn't—you couldn't.'

He slid a sidelong look at her, then, infuriatingly, relaxed back in the seat, his eyes half closed.

'I asked you a question.'

'Which you appear to have answered yourself.'

'I'd like to hear *your* answer,' she said, staring at him intently, as did the air hostess who strolled past. Claire could read what was going through the other woman's head. Who is this? Should I recognise him? Is he someone famous? She offered them a glass of champagne, which he declined with a smile of devastating charm, and then resumed his position of lazy relaxation.

'Well?' she persisted.

'If you must know,' he said on a resigned sigh, 'I did pull a few strings, now that you mention it.'

Claire gave him a killing look and said furiously, 'I don't believe it! Of all the conniving, downright *low* things I've ever heard, that takes the cake. How could you?'

'Easily enough,' he responded, deliberately misreading her accusation. 'One of my subsidiaries in New York is involved in a takeover and I decided to give the job to his company. I merely requested that Hancock handle the affair.'

She balled her fists and felt the blood rush to her head.

'Has anyone ever told you how objectionable you can be?' she hissed, with what she considered overwhelming understatement, and he appeared to give that some thought.

'Only you.' He wasn't looking in the least bit flustered, which infuriated her even more.

'You can't run people's lives for them!' she snapped angrily. 'What were you trying to prove by doing that? That you're powerful? That you can arrange everybody and everything to suit you?'

'It was for your own good,' he said, beginning to look irritable. He turned to face her better and her breath caught in her throat, her nerves prickling. He was wearing a stone-coloured shirt and his skin, in contrast, looked even more bronzed, his hair darker, his eyes more vivid. He had a knack of making everyone else seem anaemic in comparison. 'You can't cope with someone like that. You're not experienced enough.'

'I ought to go back to London right away,' Claire muttered, too alarmed by the intensity of his stare, the sheer masculinity he radiated, to react more vehemently.

'You can't.'

'Oh, I know that!' she glowered. 'I am not an idiot, though!'

'No?' He gave her a slow, lazy smile. 'Look at how long it took you to master the alarm for the manor when you were working there.'

Distracted, she replied defensively, 'You don't have an alarm, you have an early warning radar system. You need a maths degree to work it out.'

He gave her a wicked grin which she did her best to ignore. 'And don't think you can throw me off beam,' she felt compelled to add. 'I resent you treating me like a puppet. Pull a few strings, and watch me respond!'

'Why?' he demanded. 'Unless you had Hancock lined up as a marriageable opportunity. With me a no-go area, were you trying your luck elsewhere?'

'You're mad,' she threw at him.

'Good,' he said, pleased with that answer. 'Then there's no problem, is there? I did you a favour. He looked as though he could be a bit on the obnoxious side.'

He leaned back and closed his eyes and it was all she could do not to scream with frustration. The man, she thought, was a steamroller. How was it that she had never seen that before? She must have been too shellshocked by the effect he had had on her senses.

'Well, thank you,' she said sarcastically, 'O, great one. I'm so grateful to you that I'm speechless.'

It was water off a duck's back, of course. He was quite unperturbed at what he had done, and he was even less perturbed by her reaction to it, and the worst thing was that he was right. She was glad that she hadn't had to fend off any unwelcome attentions from Stephen, not that she would ever admit that in a thousand years.

It was something of a relief when the plane landed and they were in a taxi, heading for their hotel. She could genuinely lose herself in the wonderful spectacle of Paris and pretend to herself that James wasn't sitting next to her, a tantalising, threatening presence that left her weak kneed.

There was something utterly refined about Paris, with its graceful architecture and chic women hurrying through the streets. London could be breathtaking, but Paris was haughty, and Claire's eyes were round with the newness of it all by the time they arrived at the hotel.

James had obviously been before. He was recognised and treated with the servile respect given to dignitaries passing through. Claire hovered in the background, looking around her at the impressive if heavy décor, wondering whether she liked it or whether what she felt was a sort of guilty intimidation. So this was what it was like living in the lap of luxury, taking for granted the first-class flights, the first-class hotels. James barely noticed any of it.

Had Olivia been as gauche as she was? Claire wondered, and the thought of that blonde, elusive but ever-present shadow immediately made her stiffen.

James had checked them in and they followed the porter to the lift, up to the third floor, where they were shown to the two separate rooms.

Claire immediately felt a gush of relief which was not lost on him.

'Did you think that I would book us into one room?' he asked, his lips twisted into a harsh smile. 'The world is full of willing women; why do you think I would force my attentions on a reluctant party?'

'You're so flattering, James,' she answered sarcastically, offended.

His eyes narrowed. 'Realistic. Believe it or not, you haven't got the monopoly on honesty. Why is it that women love dishing out home truths but the minute the table's turned they become venomous?'

'That's a terrible generalisation.'

'Is it?' He indicated to the porter to leave their bags and gave him a tip in francs, which met with a broad smile.

'Was your wife like that?' Claire asked, continuing hurriedly when she saw the expression in his eyes. 'I mean, you never speak about her. I know you didn't

plan on my finding out about her existence, but now
that I have, why don't you talk about her?'

He gripped her forearms with his hands and his fingers
bit painfully into her. 'When I want counselling, I'll ask.
In the meanwhile, take some advice and drop the subject
of my wife.'

'Why?' Claire pursued recklessly. What did she have
to lose? She had already lost him, not that he had ever
been hers for the asking. 'Why should I tiptoe round
her memory? What was she like? Did she laugh a lot?
Was she quiet? Extrovert?'

Now that she had come right out and asked him, she
found that she was dying of curiosity. She had contained
all her questions, thinking that silence on the subject
was a form of self-defence against acknowledging how
much he had loved his wife, but why should she carry
on with that forever? He didn't mind barging back into
her life, accusing her of being a gold-digger, and then,
as if that wasn't bad enough, lecturing to her on her
stupidity in supposedly getting involved with Stephen
Hancock. What if she had been serious about Stephen?
That possibility hadn't stopped him from ruining that.
He had manipulated them both because he thought her
too damned stupid to look after herself, not that that
was any ongoing concern of his. He probably felt guilty
that he had slept with her, taken her virginity, when he
had had no intention whatsoever of making their relationship permanent. He must have known from the
start that she was gullible, not like those sophisticated
women he normally surrounded himself with, and now
he felt some kind of warped obligation to protect her
from herself.

'Why do you want to know?' he asked tightly, his dark-
fringed eyes boring into hers. Sometimes, like now, she
felt as though she was staring at a stranger. It was hard

to believe that this was the same man who had made love to her countless times, who had touched her with unhurried tenderness, who had made her laugh and made her cross. She told herself that all that had changed the minute he realised that she was no longer going to be his plaything, but deep down she knew that it had all changed the day his wife's existence had been brought out into the open.

'Would it make you feel better to know what your competition had been like?' he continued in the same unrecognisable, hard voice. 'Is that it? Do you think that if you knew what Olivia had been like, you might be able to adapt yourself a bit, make yourself a little more like what you think I want? Is that it?'

Claire couldn't believe her ears. 'Yes,' she snapped, 'that's it exactly!'

That only made him angrier, and his anger made him more frightening and remote. He shook her like a rag doll and she tried to wrench herself free of him.

'Leave me alone!' she panted, and he ignored her.

'OK,' he rasped, 'you want to know what Olivia was like? Well, I'll tell you. She was nothing like you. If you're planning on modelling yourself on her to get back into my good books now that Hancock is through the window, then you've got a long way to go.'

Claire stared at him helplessly. 'What do you mean, she was nothing like me?' she whispered in a small voice. What's wrong with me? she wanted to say.

He stared at her then let his arms drop to his sides. 'Olivia was self-assured,' he said harshly. 'She was a woman, a sophisticated, confident woman who knew what she wanted out of life and wasn't afraid to go all-out to get it.'

'And me?'

'What happened between us was a mistake,' he said roughly. 'I knew that at the time, but I couldn't resist.'

There was a pause and she could hear her heart thumping in her chest. She felt so sick that she had to reach out and support herself against the doorframe. It had seemed logical to fire all those questions at him, but she hadn't stopped to think that she mightn't like the answers.

'You went to my head like a drug,' he said, and that dark anger in his eyes was replaced by something else, something she recognised.

'Don't you dare——' she began, but she couldn't finish what she was going to say because his dark head swooped down and his mouth covered hers hungrily while his hand reached up behind her neck so that she was forced against him and she found her body curving into his, her mouth opening to receive his tongue.

With one violent movement she kicked him hard on the shin and he jerked back.

'You little...!'

Claire looked at him icily. 'So I'm a drug, am I?' she asked, clasping her arms around her body because she didn't want him to see how aroused she was. 'Well, you'll have to wean yourself off me, won't you? And shock therapy is the best.' Her voice sounded unsteady, though, and she hoped that he would put that down to anger, because however aroused she was, she was fuming. 'Is that why you got me over here? To try and get me back into bed? To make sure that Stephen wasn't around to get in your way?' A thought struck her. 'All that rubbish about him was a lie, wasn't it? Wasn't it? Well, we're here on business, so what are your plans for today? What time will we be going to see your company?'

She looked at him evenly. Less than four months ago, she would never have been able to see that handsome, hard-boned face without lighting up like a Christmas tree. From the moment she had realised that she loved him, she had made no pretence about keeping it to herself. Now, though, she was fast learning a very useful art of marshalling her features into an expressionless mask, even if her emotions were going mad under that cool surface.

'Don't be a fool,' was all he said, in a grim voice. He rubbed his shin and muttered, 'You pack one hell of a kick for someone so small.'

'Only when I have to,' Claire said, eyeing him scathingly. Not only unsophisticated, a complete buffoon in fact, but a dwarf with it. In fact, everything his tall, elegant, sophisticated wife wasn't. 'And you'd better not try anything else or you'll find my party-piece even more unimpressive.'

He grinned at her and she scowled. 'We can leave here in about an hour's time,' he said, straightening and towering over her. 'You damned vicious tigress. That should give you enough time to freshen up, unless, of course, you need a little longer? We're not due at any particular time, but I've told the managing director to expect me.'

Wasn't that, she thought, just like him? He gave orders and was obeyed. Life was something that he had under control. Well, just so long as he didn't continue to think that he had her under control as well.

'An hour should be fine,' she said, shifting her eyes away from his face to the potted plant unobtrusively occupying the corner by the lift. 'Shall I meet you in the lobby downstairs?'

He inclined his head, and she turned and walked into the bedroom, making sure to lock the door behind her. In the sanctuary of the bedroom she could be herself, could free her body from its rigid tension, give rein to the frustrating, disturbing suspicion that she could never rid herself of his power over her.

She unpacked her bag quickly, had a shower and then changed into a taupe suit, another new acquisition, which, as she stared at her reflection in the mirror, fitted her rather better than the one she had travelled in. The skirt was knee-length and flattered her small waist, and the jacket, fitting to the waist, gave her a slightly sexy look.

James didn't say a word about how she looked, but the managing director, she was blushingly flattered to see, was not so reticent. He was a short man, balding, but with an expressive face, very mobile, his eyes shrewd and dark, like a sparrow's. He took her hand and kissed it, in an antiquated gesture which Claire found rather touching, and said something to her in rapid French, which she didn't understand, but which James drily translated for her. It was a compliment, and she murmured a polite thank-you, still red-faced, back to him in her Anglicised French accent.

The rest of the day passed in a whirlwind of activity. James had arranged to meet the financial director, and vanished once she was established with the managing director and the marketing manager, both of whom, in semi-fluent English, took her through the products, their method of manufacturing, and what aspects they were hoping to emphasise in an advertising campaign.

The adverts were destined for both the newspapers and several magazines, and it was five o'clock before she realised it. They had only broken off briefly for some sandwiches in between. Her mind was buzzing with ideas, which she planned to discuss with the marketing manager the following day. Did they want something modern? Nostalgic? Evocative? Factual?

She was totally absorbed when James strode in to collect her. She read the amused smile on his face, and, in a pleasantly satisfied frame of mind, couldn't work up the energy to erect her defences, so she smiled back and said, 'It's been an enjoyable day.' Henri, the marketing manager, nodded and then addressed James in French, while Claire listened, impressed, as James replied in equally rapid French.

On the way out to the car, a chauffeur-driven Citroën which was waiting for them, she said casually, 'How's your shin?'

'Nothing,' he said with a sidelong look at her, 'that a spot of gentle massage wouldn't cure.'

'You must mention it to the hotel manager,' Claire answered calmly. 'I'm sure something could be arranged for you. I had no idea that you spoke French, by the way.'

'And German,' he replied drily, acknowledging the change of subject. 'In the business world, it pays to have a grasp of a foreign language. It's a cut-and-thrust world out there, and if you're not on your toes it's easy to get gobbled up by predators.'

'So the trick is to stay one step ahead of them all, is that it?' she asked with a wry glance. The chauffeur was holding the back door open for them, and she slipped inside, moving across so that he could sit alongside her.

It had been a long day and she was beginning to feel tired, but pleasantly so. It was easy to forget that the man sitting next to her was a threat to her wellbeing.

'Something like that,' he replied, shrugging.

'Sounds energetic and tiring,' Claire mused, leaning back against the tan leather upholstery and half closing her eyes. There was a dark partition between the front and back seats, and in the relative privacy she almost felt as though she could fall asleep. 'I can't imaging going through life always obliged to keep one step ahead of the rest of mankind.'

'That's because you're trusting,' he said lazily. 'There's a streak of the romantic in you, which is fine if you don't spend your life dealing with sharks.'

'How can I be romantic if I'm a gold-digger?' Claire said without heat.

'*Touché*,' he drawled, looking at her from under his lashes. 'A woman of contradictions.'

'And don't start flirting with me,' she said, lying back with her eyes closed. She felt too relaxed to fight, and anyway there was something teasing about his voice, nothing that she could get worked up about.

'Are you scared you might respond?'

'No,' she answered, but the corners of her mouth tilted into a smile. 'I'm scared I might cause you permanent damage.'

He laughed at that, and she felt her pulses quicken. She had been wrong. This bantering was even more dangerous than open warfare.

'Permanent damage,' he said oddly. 'Now there's a thought.' He laughed again, softly. 'As to the flirting, maybe you're right. Maybe I won't try that with you again. Maybe,' he said, 'I'll just try for the kill.'

CHAPTER NINE

TRY for the kill. James's promise echoed in Claire's head until she had to lie on the bed with her eyes shut, as if she were an invalid convalescing from some debilitating illness. Which, the thought crossed her mind, wasn't too inaccurate a comparison.

She hadn't been watching his face when he had uttered those words, she had been leaning back on the head-rest, thinking how easy it was to let his charm lower her defences and vaguely realising that she couldn't afford to let his warmth and humour, when he chose to display them, send her spinning back to square one. But she had heard the amused threat in his voice and had jerked forward to stare at him, aghast.

He had smiled at her, and then looked at her, very slowly, in that way he had, as if his eyes were eating you up. In the past, that look had been enough to send her reeling, but in the taxi it had made her mouth go dry.

'Don't even think about it,' she had said, trying to make her voice sound menacing and instead sounding uneasy and a little desperate.

'OK,' he had agreed, inspecting her with that same devastating smile. 'I won't.'

Faced with that, Claire had muttered, 'Good,' but his tone of voice had made her feel even more restless and panicky.

She might not have known of Olivia's existence until recently, that might have been a huge chunk of his life of which she had been unaware, but after months in his company she knew him well enough to know how his mind worked. He had never intended anything lasting with her, and, who knew, maybe he seriously thought that she had been after his money, but he had fancied her and he still did. She had surprised him by walking out on him and, whatever he believed of her, he wanted her back in his bed, even if it was for one night only.

The arrival of Stephen on the scene had been a temporary set-back and he had dealt with it the only way he knew how: by using his considerable power to nullify it. As far as James was concerned, problems were not to be tolerated, they were to be eliminated. It was the same rule that applied to his work as to his personal life. He could be quite ruthless, and he hadn't hesitated to use that streak in getting rid of what he saw as an unwelcome problem. It was debatable whether all that stuff he had told her about Stephen had actually been fact. She didn't think that he would have lied, but because he might not have lied, it didn't mean that he had been scrupulously truthful. Look at how he had kept her in the dark about his wife.

He had spent the rest of the journey back to the hotel chatting to her about Paris, making the taxi driver take the most convoluted way back so that he could point out various landmarks to her. In fact, making sure that she couldn't bring the conversation back to what he had said.

When they had arrived back at the hotel, and he had asked her to have dinner with him, she had been forced to accept because the expression in his eyes implied that, if she didn't, then it was because she was frightened of being alone with him. She couldn't win.

She lay on the bed and groaned. James Forrester was an exercise in determination. He hadn't needed to tell her that what he wanted, he got. It was there for her to read in the self-assurance of his smile and in the knowing, confident lift of his brows.

It was all a game to him, of course, and she had no intention of letting him retire the winner, but she would have to have her wits about her because, if she knew him, then he likewise knew her. When he looked at her he took in everything, meticulously, knowing that her coolness was only a veneer.

These eight days in Paris were going to be a war of wills. If she could survive it, then she would be able to survive anything. Anyway, once back in England she would be safe from him. There were places to run to in England and sooner or later he would get bored with the chase. She refused to entertain the possibility that she would give in.

He had arranged for them to meet in one of the hotel bars at seven-thirty.

'We could explore Paris a bit before we eat,' he had told her, his green eyes glinting, and she had replied coolly,

'If you like.' There was no point in kicking up a fuss with everything he suggested. It was a waste of effort because inevitably he got his own way, and anyway she would need to conserve her energies for more subtle attacks.

What she was going to wear she had no idea. She would have felt a little silly in one of the suits, but from his description of the restaurant the black pair of trousers would not be dressy enough.

She pulled out the dress she had worn to her sister's party and shrugged. Why not?

She spent so long thinking about him and wondering how she was going to defend herself against him that she ended up having to rush about to get dressed. She normally wore very little make-up, if any, but tonight she applied a bit of colour to her cheeks, and quite a daring shade of red lipstick. The dress needed it. It was not the sort of outfit to be worn with too much of a healthy, fresh-faced glow.

When she heard a knock on the door, she looked at it with a sudden fluttering in her chest.

'You could at least have allowed me my last thirty minutes' worth of peace,' she muttered irritably, making sure that everything was in place when she opened the door.

She opened her mouth to tell him that if he wouldn't mind waiting in the bar she would be with him shortly when her eyes opened in amazement.

'You,' she said. 'What are you doing here?' She fell back, and Stephen clearly saw that as an invitation to enter, because he walked in and looked around him, impressed.

'I knew these rooms would be nice,' he said, fingering the lacquered top of the chest of drawers, 'but this is mind-blowing, isn't it?'

'Very nice,' Claire agreed, looking at him nervously. 'What on earth are you doing here?'

'What kind of a question is that? Aren't you pleased to see me, babe?'

She looked at him warily. The last person she had expected to find on her doorstep, so to speak, was Stephen, and now that he had put the question to her she realised that she wasn't very pleased to see him at all.

He sat down and she said, 'I'm sorry, but I'm on my way out.'

'Dinner with the client?' he asked, and she nodded. 'Something like that.'

'Lucky man.' His eyes swept over her in an insolent appraisal. 'I recognise the dress. It's the same one you wore to that party your sister threw, isn't it? I couldn't take my eyes off you then. You have no idea how sexy you look in that little number. All come-hither but with a kind of schoolgirl freshness. Very appealing.'

Claire didn't like the sound of this at all, and she didn't much care for the look of him either. The amicable front she had always seen him in was gone and there was something unsettling about the way he was staring at her with those very blue eyes of his.

'Yes, well…' she hedged, wondering whether it would be overreacting to make a dash for the bedroom door. 'It's nice seeing you,' she lied, 'but if you wouldn't mind leaving, I really must…'

'I would.'

'Sorry?'

'I would mind leaving. I invested quite a bit of my time in you, not to mention a fair amount of money, what with one thing and another. The least I would expect is a bit more hospitality.'

She found that she was perspiring and she wiped the palms of her hands on her dress. She shouldn't have let him come in. She should have stayed by the door instead of walking back into the room. Sitting where he was, he could easily stop her from escaping. Then she laughed nervously to herself. What was she thinking about, *escaping*? Stephen Hancock was an acquaintance of her sister's. She had gone out with him, for heaven's sake! She must have misread what he had just said.

'How long have you been over here?' she asked, trying a different approach, the friendly one.

'Not long. A few hours.'

'On business?'

'No way. A bit of a breather before I get back to the Big Apple.' He crossed his feet at the ankles, stretching his legs out in front of him.

He was wearing a pair of jeans and a T-shirt, also in faded blue, and a pair of loafers. He looked like the average tourist, dressed for comfort, although she suspected that a closer inspection would probably reveal designer labels on everything.

'How nice for you,' she said politely. 'And have you come with anyone?'

'Oh, no, all this way just to see you.'

Oh, God, she thought, feeling a little sick, even though her mind refused to take in anything sinister behind his words. It was safer to accept what he was saying at face value.

'Well, perhaps tomorrow,' she said crisply, trying another tack, 'if you're still in town, we could...'

'Not tomorrow, Claire,' he said, standing up. 'Now. I came all this way to be with you and I'm kinda hoping you feel the same way I'm feeling.'

He moved towards her and her eyes widened with alarm.

'I thought I'd made my position absolutely clear,' she said in a high, firm voice.

'Yes, but the way I looked at it was, why would you come out with me at all if part of you didn't want something more than a load of chat and the odd meal?' He was standing in front of her now and she didn't dare meet his eyes, because there was a frantic little voice in her head telling her that she was in very hot water.

'I wouldn't have,' she stammered, 'if I had known, if I had thought...'

She felt his hands on her arms with a feeling of terrified inevitability and her blood started rushing around her veins, hot and scared.

'You don't know what you're doing,' she said weakly, squirming against him, which made him grip her harder until she had to grit her teeth together to blank out the pain.

This was getting dangerously out of control, she thought, then she almost fainted as his lips came down on hers and she found her head being pressed backwards. They stumbled and half fell on to the bed and she stuck her hands out in front of her, trying to push him away, but he was bigger than her and stronger, and in no mood to quietly retreat at the first sign of rejection.

'No...!' Claire cried out, as he covered her thighs with his leg. Her dress had ridden up and she wriggled in a frantic attempt to reinstate some semblance of modesty.

'Come on, babe,' he groaned, 'don't tell me you don't fancy me. Why else would you have gone out with me?'

'I didn't think *I* was being bought, along with the food!'

He wasn't listening. He nipped her neck with his teeth, then her stomach clenched as his hand descended over her breast and he caressed it, breathing quickly and heavily as his fingers found her nipple and he began rubbing it.

Claire pushed as hard as she could, no longer caring how much her dress had ridden up, but it was only when she dug her fingernails into his sides that he withdrew with a sharp cry of pain.

This is it, she thought, terrified. I've read the books, I've seen the movies, and digging my fingernails into this man won't turn him into a quivering wreck. They were both breathing heavily and they stared at each other.

'Get off me!' she ordered, deciding to strike while the iron was hot, and she struggled up, tugging her dress down and half expecting him to jump at her and renew his attack. 'Get out!' she said. 'How could you? How *could* you?'

'All right!' He eyed her with hostility, but at least he was listening to common sense. 'What did you expect?' he demanded aggressively, and she took a precautionary step back as he took one towards her.

'Out!' she yelled and at the same time she heard James's voice from the other side of the door, then banging.

'What the hell's going on in there?'

She sprinted across the room and flung open the door.

'He...!' she broke out, turning to stare at Stephen, who had moved towards the door but couldn't get out because James was blocking it.

James's eyes raked over her quickly, then they turned to Stephen and she heard a desperate whimper, then everything started spinning around and she felt herself sliding into unconsciousness.

When she next opened her eyes she was lying on the bed, and her first instinct was to stand up and make a bolt for the door.

James held her down and said soothingly, as if he was speaking to a child, 'He's gone. The bastard's gone!'

'Thank God.' She subsided back on to the pillow and closed her eyes tight, then she reopened them and looked straight into James's face. Underneath that consoling exterior he was as mad as hell, and she wondered what on earth he had to be mad about! She groaned and put her hand to her eyes, trying to block out the memory of Stephen all over her. She knew now that she hadn't been in any real danger, he had stopped when he had finally got the message, but at the time she had been really frightened, scared with every last ounce of blood in her.

'What did you do to him?' she asked, and James leaned over her.

'I should have knocked his block off,' he said tautly, 'but as it was I only got the satisfaction of shoving him out of the room because you damn well fainted. What the hell did you think you were doing letting him get into your bedroom? Didn't I warn you about him? Didn't it even cross your mind that you can't just open your bedroom door to men and then expect them to behave themselves?'

'Stop shouting at me,' Claire said unsteadily. 'I don't feel very well. You were right about him, all right, I admit it, but I don't need to have salt rubbed into the wound. How did I know that he was going to...to...?' She couldn't get it out. What he had done to her was so distasteful that even describing it stuck in her throat and made her want to retch.

She closed her eyes and a few tears squeezed themselves out even though she really didn't want to cry, did she. He hadn't actually *done* anything to her, after all. It could have been much worse. That thought made her feel even sicker and more tearful and she sniffed loudly, grateful for James's presence, the way he was pulling her against him and stroking her hair with his hand.

'You're a silly little fool,' he murmured brokenly. He curled his fingers into her hair and pressed her face into his neck, at which she began sobbing loudly. 'I should have wrung his neck,' he continued tightly. 'No fear, though, I'll make sure that bastard pays for what he did. I'll make sure he loses his job. I have contacts all over the world. A word in the right ear and he'll be eating bread and butter from now on.'

'No, don't do that,' she said. It was very soporific being stroked by him. He had strong hands and she loved the way they felt caressing her hair. She realised how much she desperately missed being touched by him, and not just in a sexual way. She just loved the feel of his body. Stephen was already beginning to recede from her mind. 'It was horrible, but he wasn't going to...to go

the whole way with me,' she said with a catch in her
voice. He was caressing her neck now and it felt glorious.
'I mean,' she continued, wondering what she meant. Her
mind was going very fuzzy; she couldn't seem to get her
thoughts straight at all. 'I mean he just misread the situation, and perhaps I was a little to blame. I shouldn't
have gone out with him. You're right, I was naïve.' He
was kissing her face, light little kisses that made her feel
quite faint. She raised her face to his like a flower up-
turned to the sun, her eyes still closed. This was making
her feel languorous and she eased herself back on to the
pillows, hoping that he wouldn't take his hands off her,
which he didn't.

She forgot about her fight, about the battle of wills.

'You weren't to blame,' he rasped, kicking his shoes
off and lying alongside her. 'Men like that assume that
paying for a meal entitles them to whatever they want
from a woman.'

'Most women would probably realise that from the
start,' Claire said gloomily. 'They would either go out
with him knowing what he wanted, because they wanted
it as well, or else they would tell him to get lost from
the start, which is what I should have done.'

'Why didn't you?' he asked huskily.

'Good question.'

He stroked her shoulders, then slowly contoured her
body with his hand, and she sighed.

'It wasn't because you were attracted to him.'

'Is that a question or a statement of fact?' She looked
at him through lowered lashes and he flushed darkly.

'I'd like it to be a statement of fact.'

'All right,' she agreed, and he frowned, not liking her
easy compliance. There was a brooding intimacy in his
eyes, a possessiveness that made her toes curl and she
smiled. Her mind felt sluggish, but not so sluggish that

she didn't realise that this was a dangerous situation, a deliberate arousal.

She was poised on the brink of surrender and the thought of it wasn't frightening her, it was exciting her. She opened her eyes fully and looked at him. He groaned and muttered savagely, 'Tell me that I'm the only one you want.'

'You are,' she admitted with a sigh and he bent his head towards hers, his mouth taking hers in a fierce kiss. She wound her arms around his neck and kissed him back with a desperate hunger.

His hand slipped behind her; he unzipped her dress from behind, pulling it down, and she wriggled to accommodate him.

'Why do I feel this way about you?' he asked against her skin.

He had earlier discarded his jacket. Now he discarded the rest of his clothes and she watched him, fascinated, as if she had never seen him naked before. She looked at the firm, hard outlines of his body, the broad shoulders, the lean hips, the long legs with their sprinkling of dark hair. He had a body that was engineered for seduction. Everything about it was sexy, and she couldn't wait to feel it against her.

She pulled herself free of her underclothes and sighed with pleasure as their bodies met. Her breasts seemed to have swelled in anticipation of his caress and she offered them up to him, lying back as his mouth closed over one nipple and his hands massaged the fullness of her breasts. He sucked at one, then the other, and her legs parted, inviting him to explore her.

His lips trailed a path along her stomach, to her navel and then further to the warm moistness which sent a sweet electric shock through her.

She couldn't wait. It seemed like years since she had last slept with him and now wasn't the time for leisurely foreplay. She urged him up and as he thrust into her she moved against him, their bodies moving into a rhythm which they had perfected together.

It seemed ludicrous to think that she had ever contemplated leaving this man. Everything about him fulfilled her. She remembered that she had felt very strongly about being used, but she couldn't summon up those principles which had been the basis of that feeling.

She wouldn't think too hard about all that, she decided with a mixture of sadness and resignation. She loved him, didn't she? What was the point of torturing herself by running away from the realisation that he was the only man who could ever give her what she needed?

Later, as they lay on the bed, she turned to him and said with a little laugh, 'What about dinner? Had you booked anywhere?'

He smiled wryly and kissed the corners of her mouth. 'I hadn't, as it happens, but somehow I don't think they would have kept our table if I had, do you? It's gone eleven. Are you hungry?'

She shook her head. 'No, but I suspect I'll be ravenous tomorrow morning.'

'Yes, you will,' he agreed, teasing her nipple with his finger and smiling as it hardened in ready response. 'I've seen you in one of those morning-after states. Not a pretty sight.'

She giggled and then sighed as his finger found the other nipple.

'We could always get room service,' he suggested, and she murmured something incomprehensible because her brain was ceasing to function as his fingers found other areas to explore. 'Or else,' he said huskily, 'it could wait.'

And wait it did, until the following morning when they sat in bed with a huge tray in front of them and tucked into hot croissants, flaky and buttery, small sultana and walnut rolls, fresh fruit and masses of coffee.

'You know that you've won, don't you?' she said with her head averted so that he couldn't see how much it upset her to think that her desperate love would never be returned.

'Win? Lose? This isn't a game,' he muttered, pulling her beside him. 'If I could offer you marriage and guarantee that it would last, then I would.'

'But for you that's an unrepeatable experience,' she filled in lightly.

'What do you want me to say to that? We've been over all this before, haven't we? I've been married once, it ended in tears, and I have no intention of repeating the experience, and I'm too fond of you to set you up in a position to be hurt.'

And where do you think I am now? she wanted to ask him, but he wouldn't think along those lines at all. Without the ties of marriage, she was a free agent. When they parted company they would do so without bitterness, because if *he* could then he wouldn't understand that she couldn't.

'You're so considerate,' she said, and he didn't answer. 'She really meant a lot to you, didn't she?'

'Let's put it this way: I tried my hand at marriage and it ended in tragedy. How much more clearly can I put it? I realise that according to certain gossip columns I'm something of an eligible bachelor, but I'd make a lousy husband. I'm not what you're looking for, I'm just not into playing happy families. You're a romantic, Claire. Do you think that I don't know that? You believe in happy-ever-after, and I don't.'

'There's nothing wrong with that. There's nothing wrong with wanting a family. You've told me that marriage isn't for you, but don't you want children?' Claire asked, and he shrugged.

'Olivia was pregnant when she died,' he said in a flat voice, and she looked at him, horrified.

'I'm sorry. I had no idea. How dreadful for you. How far in the pregnancy was she?'

'Four and a half months.'

'How awful. You never said...'

'Very few people know,' he conceded, which, she thought, was better than giving her another lecture on how unnecessary he felt it was to share his past with her, or anything else of importance for that matter.

'I see.' It was patently clear. His pregnant wife had died and left a legacy of disillusionment in him that could never be dispelled.

'Do you?' he asked in a gentle voice. 'I doubt it.'

'Will you never marry?'

'One day, maybe, who knows? To someone who isn't looking for the whole romantic bit.'

'Does such a woman exist?' She didn't expect him to answer that, but he did.

'Of course. For some women marriage is as much a social convenience as anything else; for others it's companionship.'

Gayle. She had no idea why that should have sprung, uninvited, into her head, but it did. He had known Gayle for a long time, hadn't he? They were good friends, good enough for him to set her up in his cottage in the grounds of the manor. And she was a career woman, someone who was into high tech, into city life, not into lazy walks in summer and nights spent sitting in front of a log fire in winter. Is she your type? Is she the woman you'll turn to when you want the social convenience of having a partner? She wanted to ask him, but her reluctance to hear his answer silenced her.

'But that doesn't mean that I'm not addicted to you,' he said in a huskier voice. 'I want you so badly that sometimes I think that it's driving me crazy. It's selfish of me, I know, and I give you my word that if you want to walk out on this relationship right now then I won't try and stop you.'

That should have set her mind at rest but all it succeeded in doing was to make her want to burst into tears all over again. He was being as direct as he possibly could be and she wondered whether she wouldn't have preferred a few white lies, because she already knew that she was going to stay with him for as long as he would have her. She didn't think that she could relive those long, desolate hours spent thinking that she would never see him again, never share anything with him again. One day, she knew, she would have to, but not yet. When that time came, she would cope with it.

'You tried to stop me before,' she pointed out, and he reddened.

'Did I?' he asked roughly, then swore under his breath. 'OK, I might have been a bit unfair, but you have my word this time. No pursuit.'

'Can I think about it?'

'No.'

'In that case,' she whispered, 'I'll be a sucker for punishment.'

He relaxed and smiled, kissing her lips lightly but persuasively.

Jackie'll kill me, she thought, and Karen's going to be stunned and I know I'll end up miserable when he does finally call it a day, but he's the breath in my body, and why do without him when I can have him just a little bit longer?

They said that absence made the heart grow fonder and now there seemed to be an edge to their passion, an intensity that hadn't been here before. She was sure she wasn't imagining it. Maybe because everything was out in the open, they were both savouring each other because the limitations of their relationship had been laid on the table and they both knew that sooner or later what they were enjoying so fiercely now would one day be water under the bridge.

At work, he was utterly professional, but all the time she was aware of a silent game being played between them, apparent in the occasional smouldering, sidelong look, in the way he brushed against her, in the way he held her eyes just that bit longer than was necessary. No one else noticed it but she found it thrilling, like an illicit enjoyment.

And in the nights they made love until every thought was driven from her brain.

They returned to England and brilliant weather. The weather men were at it again, churning out statistics about the extraordinary heat and talking about the greenhouse effect.

There was a conspiracy, Claire decided two weeks later, to keep her in this euphoric state of mind. The weather was splendid, her sister was out of the country so there was no outside pressure being put on her to do the sensible thing, and she couldn't get enough of James. It was like riding the crest of a wave, dangerous, exhilarating, filling her with wild adrenalin.

The one thing she refused to do, however, was move back into the cottage. Apart from anything else, Gayle was still there. Claire had not mentioned her thoughts about her to James, but time hadn't dimmed them any. He might not be sleeping with the tall blonde at the moment, indeed he might never have slept with her, but that didn't mean that old friends would not some day become lovers, and more. She knew, as she had always known, that he had slept with women before her, but none of them had ever seemed more threatening than Gayle King.

'I can find her somewhere else to stay,' James murmured. It was after eight but bright and warm, and they were sitting in the grounds of the manor, under the shade of a tree which rustled above them in the slight breeze. 'I want you closer to me.' He slipped his hand under her blouse and she quivered in response.

But she held her ground. Somehow she didn't care for the thought of moving back into the cottage. Sharing the house with Karen had given her a degree of independence which common sense told her that she would need one day.

She noticed that he had not volunteered to share his house with her, and she was tempted to point that out, teasingly, but she didn't. He might think that she was angling for the position of lady of the manor, despite his blunt refusal to entertain the idea, and anyway, ever since they had returned from Paris she had preferred not to dwell on the short-lived nature of their relationship. The subject of Olivia was never reopened and there was no way that she would ever put herself in the position of being accused of trying to engineer marriage.

It was exactly four weeks to the day after they returned from Paris, on another one of those mornings that promised yet more fine, sunny weather, that reality came crashing down around her.

She should have guessed sooner, of course, but she had been so caught up in him that she hadn't put two and two together until her periods were almost ten days late. Then, in a panic, she rushed out and bought one of those pregnancy testing kits and waited, in a state of nervous tension, for the results. But she knew, deep down, what the result would be even before proof positive was in front of her.

She was pregnant.

CHAPTER TEN

IT WAS one thing knowing, just *knowing* that she was pregnant. It was quite another to be staring at confirmation of it. She didn't know whether to laugh or cry, or both, and after a few minutes of doing neither she quickly disposed of the used kit and went downstairs.

Karen was there, rustling around, getting ready for work. They normally had a cup of coffee and some toast together and then she would get a lift in to the office with Karen. She was so disorientated that she couldn't think straight, and her hands were trembling as she slipped on her tracksuit and then rushed down to the kitchen to find the coffee made and the toast buttered. A feeling of nausea swept over her and then a deep, burning excitement filled her until she wanted to laugh out loud.

She was having James's baby! It seemed incredible, and she had to resist the temptation to rush back up the stairs and disentangle the little tube from the bin where it lay carefully concealed under screwed-up tissue paper.

Karen was staring at her as though she had gone mad, and she said, frowning, 'What's the matter with you? You can't be *this* happy at seven-thirty on a work morning.'

'I'm not feeling terribly well, actually,' Claire said, smiling. 'I won't be going to work.'

'You don't look ill.'

'Stomach problems—must have eaten something.' She tried not to grin too broadly at that one.

'Sure you don't mean that you need to do some shopping?' Karen looked at her suspiciously, biting into the toast while Claire poured herself some apple juice from the fridge.

'Would I do that?'

'You might.' Karen stood up, still eating what was left of the toast, and washing it down with some coffee. 'It's not unheard of.'

'Tell Tony I'll be in tomorrow, won't you?' Claire asked, smiling like an idiot.

She was still grinning when she shut the door and tentatively walked towards the telephone.

Funny, she thought, how five minutes could change the course of your life. One minute she was locked into a stalemate relationship with James, the next she was here, pregnant, and life from where she was sitting looked absolutely marvellous.

She dialled James's number.

Of course, it was all totally unexpected, the result of that one night of passion in Paris when neither of them had used contraception, but it was still wonderful, heavenly. She was carrying *his* child! She touched her stomach and felt a great deal of wonder.

The telephone rang three times and then James's secretary answered.

Everything had been going so well between them. He was going to be over the moon about this. She just *knew* it. How could he possibly be cynical about his baby? He would realise that Olivia was a tragedy that belonged to the past and that this new life beginning now, inside her, was their future.

'Hang on a sec, Claire, I'll just connect you.' Elaine was James's secretary and over the months she and Claire had built up an easy rapport over the telephone. She chatted away about this and that and Claire half listened, too excited to offer much by way of reply.

Her parents would be overjoyed, of course. Surprised, but once they met James they would see that everything was going to be fine. Her mind took off on another tangent and she began to wonder whether it would be a boy or a girl. Who would it look like?

She heard James's voice on the other end of the line and her fingers coiled around the telephone wire.

'James, it's me.'

'I know,' he said drily, 'Elaine forewarned me.'

'How are you?'

'Much the same as I was when I saw you last night. Why? Do you know something that I don't?'

I do, as a matter of fact, she wanted to say. 'Are you sitting down?'

Her stomach was going into tight, hard little knots and she could hardly wait to tell him her spectacular news.

'Yes,' he said, and there was a hint of wariness in his voice now.

'Good. Because I've got something to tell you.'

There was silence and she took a deep breath, then said in a rush, 'Guess what! I'm pregnant.'

Even in silence it was possible to discern meaning. Some silences were comfortable, like the silence between old friends, some were fraught with anticipation, like the silence between lovers. This silence stretched between them, taut and thick, and she felt the first sharp ebb of her new-found excitement.

'Are you still there?' she asked, trying hard to sound light-hearted.

'You can't be.'

'What do you mean?' Dismay was beginning to set in and it was like cold, clammy fingers crawling over her.

'We took precautions,' he said patiently.

'Not in Paris. Not on that first night.'

'I don't believe this.'

'And from the sound of it, you don't much like it either,' Claire whispered. The clammy fingers had wrapped themselves around her body and had managed to reach deep inside her, so that she felt cold all over.

'This is impossible. I can't talk about this over the phone. Where are you?'

'Whether you talk to me face to face or over the phone doesn't change the fact that I'm having your baby.'

'Dammit, Claire!'

'I should have known what to expect from you.' She didn't feel dismayed now. She felt utterly desolate.

'You spring this thing on me and expect what...?'

'I wish I'd never told you. I wish I'd walked out of your life.'

'Well, you have and you didn't.'

She heard something buzz in his office, another line, and he said to her, 'Look, I have a meeting at eleven. It's important. I'll be down as soon as I can after that. We have to sort this one out.'

'Sure,' Claire said stiffly, but her mind was working frantically. Sort this one out? What did he mean? Abortion? She would have to leave, and quickly. She could go to Jackie's place. She was still out of the country, in Australia for two months because Tom was over there on business and they had decided that two months was too long for them to be apart. She had the key to her sister's house.

She was feeling sick, sick and disillusioned, with a depth of disillusionment that would never go. It would haunt her until the day she died. He didn't want this baby, he had as good as said so, and she had been an utter fool to have expected anything other than that from him. He hadn't been joking when he had told her that he wasn't into playing happy families. He had been deadly serious. The grave error of judgement had been on her part, in thinking that this baby would represent anything to him other than a huge, unwanted complication.

She telephoned Karen at work and tried not to sound as distressed as she felt as she told her that she wasn't going to be to work for a few days, that she was going to her sister's, that James might call round and in no circumstances should she tell him where she, Claire, was. There was panic in her voice as she said that, but Karen accepted it easily enough, only saying that if something was wrong she wanted to be the first to help.

She moved quickly after that phone call. Some clothes in a case, a few books, a photo album, then a taxi up to London. James would never find her, of that she was certain. He knew of her sister's existence, but he didn't know where she lived and he didn't know her married name. Not that that would have helped, since they were ex-directory.

The only link to her was Karen, who had sworn secrecy. Not even Tony had her sister's address. When she had first started working for him, she had given the house in Reading as her point of contact, and had never bothered to change it, even after she had moved into the cottage. It had never before occurred to her how easy it would be simply to vanish, to disappear off the face of the earth, but to all intents and purposes she had vanished out of James's life, for good.

It was only later that she thought about the ramifications of her flight.

Nothing would ever take away the deep pleasure it gave her to be pregnant, but realistically she knew that life from here on in was not going to be a bed of roses. Her

child would have no father, because there was no way
that she was going to contact James. She neither wanted
an abortion nor did she want him to feel obligated to
her in any way. The euphoria which had overwhelmed
her when she had first discovered her pregnancy had been
replaced by a corrosive cynicism. He would never be
happy about this child, and she was not about to become
a noose around his neck.

Then there was the question of her family and friends.
So far she hadn't breathed a word of her condition to
anyone. She had spoken to Tony, to tell him that she
had left, vaguely attributing her sudden departure to un-
foreseen family problems, which was near enough the
truth for her not to feel too horribly guilty. She had said
the same to Karen, who had, by now, probably put two
and two together and figured out the whole sorry mess
anyway. And as for her parents—well, she hadn't even
called them at all. They still thought that she was happily
ensconced in Reading, doing all the fun things normal
young girls did. Sooner or later she would have to say
something, and she knew that it would have to be sooner
rather than later. They deserved that, even if they would
be disappointed in her. Their sheltered, uncomplicated
little girl who had never given them any trouble with
boys, pregnant by a man they had never even heard of,
far less met.

At least, she thought fiercely and protectively, the baby
will be a product of love; and that, over the next two
days, afforded her some degree of satisfaction.

She also knew that pretty soon she would have to tackle
the problem of finding another job and she wondered
whether she shouldn't simply return to her parents' home
and find work down there. It smacked a little of taking
the easy way out, but she had left her girlish dreams
behind forever. Now was no time to build castles in the

air. The knight in shining armour had turned out to be a tarnished mockery of the real thing. At least, with her parents next to her, lending her their support, she wouldn't have to cope with loneliness on top of everything else.

She was sitting on the sofa in the lounge, with a book on her lap but really staring vacantly past it, thinking over and over what she should do, when the doorbell rang.

At ten-thirty at night, in London, there was no chance that she was going to throw open the door to whoever might be lurking on the doorstep. She slipped the chain through the catch and slowly opened it, just enough to get a glimpse of whoever was outside.

'You!' she said. Her body felt as though it had been plugged into a socket and suddenly switched into furious life.

'Open this door.'

It wasn't a polite request, it was a command, and that galvanised her into anger. She pushed closed the door, frantic to double-lock it, but he had wedged his foot into it, so she fell back and said coldly, 'What are you doing here? How did you find me?' He looked dark and dishevelled and furious.

'Open this door,' he said by way of response, 'or I'll break it down.'

'Go away.'

He didn't answer. He gave the door a shove with his shoulder and she stepped back, alarmed and panic-stricken. He wouldn't really break it down, she thought, he was bluffing. But he wasn't. He gave another shove, this time with his shoulder, and the chain snapped as though it was made of papier mâché. He swept into the room, a tall, forbidding force, and she turned to run, not getting anywhere because his hand clamped on to her arm, biting into her.

'You bloody little fool,' he snarled. 'What do you mean by running out like that? I should throttle you.'

'Throttle me! Take your hand off me this instant or I'll scream the place down! I'll have everyone running here from a fifty-mile radius to see what's going on! I don't want you here; I want you to leave me alone!'

He pulled her, protesting, to the sofa and gave her a little push on to it.

'I've been out of my mind looking for you,' he bit out, 'and now that I've found you there's no way that you're running out.'

'Who told you where I was?'

'I had to crawl to that Hancock bastard,' he said, 'crawl! I was at my wit's end to get your sister's address. I knew you'd be here, hiding!'

She looked up at him stubbornly. 'So you found me, Sherlock Holmes. Big deal. We still have nothing to say to each other.'

'You're having my baby! And we have nothing to say to each other?' His voice was savage.

'That's right!' she shouted. 'Nothing! Which is about all you had to say on the subject first time round! So why the change of heart, James? Have you come trooping along here to persuade me to get rid of it? The whole world knows that the last thing you want in your life is a baby!'

'Well, the whole damn world's wrong!'

The silence after that was resounding. He sat down heavily next to her and raked his fingers through his hair. His anger had vanished, he looked like a man standing in front of a two-thousand-strong audience, about to give a speech on a subject he knew nothing about.

'You little fool,' he murmured, looking at her from under lowered lashes. 'No, I'm the fool. I can't blame you for running away, not when I acted the way I did. When you told me that you were pregnant, I was shocked, I admit it. Dammit, woman, what could you expect?'

'I wonder,' Claire said bitterly and he frowned.

'Don't say that. Not in that tone of voice. I don't want to hear that disillusionment there, even though, if it is, I have no one but myself to blame.' He reached out to cup her face. 'Please, marry me, Claire. That's what I should have said to you a long time ago.'

'I can't,' she replied, not meeting his green-eyed stare. 'I can't spend my life living in your wife's shadow and I can't marry you thinking that the only reason you proposed was for the sake of the baby.'

'Listen to me,' he murmured roughly, 'and don't interrupt until I'm finished. I know I gave you the impression that no one could replace my wife, but I was protecting myself. I'd spent so long not wanting involvement, steering clear of it in fact, that it had become a habit that I couldn't break. When you came along, something about you fascinated me, excited me, and I never stopped to question whether what I was feeling was anything more than passion. You see, I thought I was damn well unassailable, that I'd learnt from my marriage to Olivia...'

'...not to trust anyone,' Claire whispered, and he silenced her by placing his hand over her mouth.

'Yes, not to trust anyone,' he agreed, letting his hand drop to hers, stroking her wrist with his thumb, an absent-minded gesture that made her head spin. 'You see, I never loved my wife. In fact, in the end, I didn't even like her. I married her because she was pregnant and I couldn't bring myself to walk out on my own flesh and blood.'

Claire looked at him in shock and she would have spoken, but he carried on. The release of pent-up emotion, feelings buried for too long, could be cathartic, and the burden of his past was one which he was lifting from his shoulders.

'We'd been casually seeing each other for a few months, but I knew her for long enough to realise that I didn't love her and I never would. It was a fling that should never have been started in the first place and I very quickly realised that, but once we had slept together she became obsessed with me. She began discussing marriage, even though I told her that I wasn't interested, and when I refused to back down, she broke the bombshell. She was pregnant, and if I didn't marry her she would make sure that every scandal sheet in the country knew that I was running out on my responsibilities. I didn't give a damn about what the newspapers had to say about me, but I wasn't about to run out on my child, even though a child was the last thing I'd wanted when I started seeing her. Of course, she realised almost immediately that the whole thing was going to be a disaster and in the weeks before her death, she became reckless, she started seeing other men. You see, she realised that she hadn't loved me at all. We were totally imcompatible and we both knew it.' He sighed heavily. 'After that I made sure that no woman ever got close. Then you came along, with your glorious innocence and faith in human nature, and I found my principles being gradually eaten away at the edges, until all that carefully nurtured cynicism was a pile of ashes.'

'You could have fooled me,' Claire said wryly.

'That was the object of the exercise.' His eyes were ironic. 'In some recess in my mind I thought that if I could fool you then I might succeed in fooling myself as well. When you walked out on me, I felt as though I'd been punched in the stomach. I never expected you to leave. I thought I'd explain about Olivia, what needed explaining at any rate, and things could continue as normal. Call it convenient blindness. When I found out that you were seeing someone I went berserk. You'd said you loved me but that seemed like a long time ago, and suddenly I wasn't so sure of you. You'd gone, you were seeing that man, maybe even sleeping with him, and I couldn't stand the thought of it. Worse than that, I couldn't stand the thought of how much it meant to me. After Olivia's death, I had decided that women were opportunists, and I'd spent years carefully constructing my life around that assumption. Yet here I was, going mad because of you.' His voice was hoarse and she smiled, her eyes teasing.

'Good.'

'You witch,' he said ruefully, 'I suppose you know what I'm saying here, don't you?'

'Do I? Tell me, what are you saying?'

'I love you, Claire,' he murmured, and her ears sang. 'I've always loved you, even when the possibility of that never crossed my mind. I love everything about you, dammit, and I want you back.' She felt a fierce, wild exultation and it showed in her eyes as she looked up at him, no longer under pressure to try and hide her adoration.

'Will you marry me?' he repeated soberly, and she nodded.

'But first,' she said, 'tell me about Gayle. I've spent hours agonising about her.'

'Gayle? Oh, there's nothing to tell there. We're friends, believe it or not. Were you jealous?'

'What do you think?'

'You never showed it,' he said, his eyes glinting. 'And after all the trouble I went to arranging for her to have the cottage, knowing that you two would meet at some point in time, waiting for you to come running back to me.'

'You beast!'

'You only have yourself to blame. Mind you,' he said, and he stroked her neck, 'one good thing did come out of her presence. She warned me about Stephen Hancock, not that you paid a scrap of attention to me.'

'I should have.' She remembered that night in Paris with some distaste.

'I guess I laid it on a bit thick. I was furious when you took no notice. I thought that exposing him to you would be the card up my sleeve, and instead you ignored me. I could have killed you, or him, or the whole damn world.'

She laughed and he made a husky sound, pulling her against him, seeking and finding her mouth with his, while his hand rested lightly on her stomach.

'You have no idea what it does to me knowing that you're carryng my child,' he said in a low, unsteady voice. 'I can't imagine what ever possessed me to think that I wasn't a family man. Do you know, when you told me over the phone that you were pregnant, I was speechless, but at the same time I felt an enormous, incredible joy. That,' he said, looking right into her eyes, 'was until you hung up and then took flight. When I discovered that you had gone and that wretched roommate of yours wouldn't breathe a word, never mind giving me your sister's telephone number, I was in a blind panic. I'd never felt anything like it before. I would have searched every single house, flat, bedsit, whatever, in London if it took me the rest of my life. I knew that I couldn't live without you.' He slipped his hand under her shirt and caressed her stomach. 'It doesn't show,' he murmured.

'It will soon.'

'I can't wait. I want the whole world to know that you're mine and that you're pregnant with our baby.'

He unzipped her trousers and slipped his hand underneath the lacy edge of her underwear, cupping her down there gently.

'I need you so badly, woman,' he groaned and she pulled his head to hers, sprinkling kisses on his face.

'You don't know how long I've waited to hear those words,' she murmured breathlessly, moving against him. 'I seem to have spent so long torn between hope and despair and in the end there was only the despair. When I came up here and I thought that that was it between us, that I was forever out of your reach, even if you bothered to look—well, it was a nightmare. I missed being mad at you, wondering what was going to become of us! Silly, isn't it?'

'I think it's called love,' he whispered, his eyes dark with passion, 'something I find I can't do without. Where, by the way, is your sister?'

'In Australia.'

'Good,' he murmured with a crooked smile and an expression that left her in no doubt as to what he was thinking. 'Because we have some catching up to do——' he stroked her stomach lovingly '—my dearest wife to be and mother.'